D0507734

351687446

THE RUNAWAY HEART

Rescued by fate from a repulsive marriage, Karina finds herself strangely drawn to Garland Holt, who is convinced that his money is the attraction. Before Karina can prove this is not so Garland's fantastic jade collection disappears. Called upon now to prove not only her love but also her honesty, Karina sees the world tumbling about her. This is the vivid story of a girl who discovers that the pieces of a broken heart can build themselves into a dream come true...

THE RUNAWAY HEART

The Runaway Heart

by

Barbara Cartland

Magna Large Print Books
Long Preston, North Yorkshire,
BD23 4ND, England.

British Library Cataloguing in Publication Data.

Cartland, Barbara
  The runaway heart.

A catalogue record of this book is
available from the British Library

ISBN 0-7505-1814-6

First published in Great Britain by Herbert Jenkins Ltd.

Copyright © Barbara McCorquodale, 1961

Cover illustration © Ben Turner by arrangement with
Rupert Crew Ltd.

The moral right of the author has been asserted

Published in Large Print 2002 by arrangement with
Cartland Promotions, care of Rupert Crew Ltd.

Magna Large Print is an imprint of Library Magna Books Ltd.

Printed and bound in Great Britain by
T.J. (International) Ltd., Cornwall, PL28 8RW

CHAPTER ONE

There was a gentle knock on the door, which was opened immediately.

'Are you there?' a voice breathed, hardly above a whisper.

'Of course,' a man's voice replied. 'Who else did you think it was?'

'Oh, do be careful. Don't speak so loudly.'

The girl's reply was agitated. Now she pulled the door wider and the man outside stepped forward and put his arm around her shoulders.

'Don't worry, Karina,' he said. 'It is quite all right. There's no one about and it's nearly dark, anyway. Stop trembling. Everything will be all right.'

'I suppose it will,' she answered almost with a sob. 'Aunt Margaret is in the library with Uncle Simon. They are reading the newspapers, as they always do at this time of the evening.'

'And Cyril? Where's Cyril?'

'He has gone to the stables. He shouldn't be back for at least an hour.'

'Then what are you worrying about?' the man asked. 'Come on! Let's get it over. Where's your luggage?'

9

'It's just at the top of the stairs,' she said. 'I didn't dare bring it any farther in case somebody heard me.'

'All right, I'll get it.'

The man turned and ran up the narrow stairway and a moment later came down again carrying a heavy suitcase. He put it down at the girl's feet, smiled at her and asked:

'What are you bringing with you? Bricks? That's what it feels like.'

'I thought I'd better pack everything,' she murmured; but he did not hear her because already he had gone up the stairs again, this time to reappear with two suitcases, one in each hand.

They were such a burden that he found it difficult to negotiate the narrow staircase, which, covered in linoleum, was exactly the kind of staircase that could be found in the back quarters of every large country house.

'Is that the lot?' he asked a little breathlessly.

'Yes … no, there's my hat-box,' the girl cried. 'But I'll get that. You go ahead with the suitcases.'

She didn't wait for his reply, but ran up the stairs swiftly and gracefully, to come down them much more slowly, a large hat-box in her hand.

In fact it seemed unnaturally large because she was such a tiny person. Even in the

10

dusky gloom it was possible to see the shining fairness of her hair and the wide blue eyes set in a little oval face. In her prim woollen dress and tweed coat she looked like a schoolgirl, and the thought must have struck the man returning for her, for he stood still a moment and said:

'You are quite sure you are nearly twenty-one? I don't particularly want to spend a few years in prison for abducting someone under sixteen.'

Karina laughed.

'Don't be ridiculous, Cousin Felix! You know you were asked to my twentieth birthday party last year.'

'But I didn't come,' he said.

'No, you didn't come,' she sighed. 'All the relations were asked and only the very old and very dull ones turned up.'

'Well, if you're nearly twenty-one, you certainly don't look it,' he said. 'Come on, wide eyes, let's hurry to the car before someone discovers it in the drive and wonders why it is waiting there.'

Karina picked up the hat-box, which she had put down at the foot of the staircase while she talked to Felix. Lifting the suitcases, Felix Mainwaring preceded her out of the door, along a narrow cinder path which skirted the back premises and, twisting through some rhododendron bushes, came out on to the wide, oak-bordered

11

avenue which led to the main gates of Letchfield Park.

A long, grey Bentley was standing a few yards from them. It seemed to melt into the dusk and the dark shadows under the trees so that for the moment it seemed unreal, a figment, Karina thought, of her imagination.

And then she was in the front seat, Felix had piled in the suitcases and the hat-box, the lights flashed into life, there was a sudden purr of the engine and the headlights picked out the trunks of the trees standing sentinel on either side of the drive, and they were away.

She gave a little gasp, clenching her hands together. There were the gates ahead, with a lodge on either side of them. Supposing, just supposing, they were stopped? What would happen if old Mrs Withers, who had lived in one of them for nearly forty years, came hurrying out? Or if old Abbey, the groom, who had retired only last year after sixty years of service, should come and speak to them and say that she was wanted back at the house?

'Your uncle wants you, Miss Karina.'

She could almost hear him saying it.

The gates were open! Open! The car was moving through them. They were on the road, moving swiftly and ever more swiftly over smooth tarmac, a signpost, white as a ghostly hand, pointing the way to London.

'Well, how do you feel now?'

Felix turned his head for a fleeting second to smile at her.

'I ... I can't believe it's true. Have I really ... escaped? Won't they ... fetch me back?'

'They will try,' he said. 'But you are your own mistress. Or you will be in a few weeks. Why didn't you run away before, you little fool?'

'I didn't know where to go,' Karina answered. 'Besides, I didn't want to hurt them. They have always been kind to me. It is the only home I can ever remember.'

'Kind!' Felix Mainwaring made the word sound both scornful and indignant. 'So kind that they were determined to keep you as their daughter-in-law, married to their mentally deficient son!'

Karina gave a little sob.

'Oh, no, Cousin Felix, that's not quite fair. Cyril's quite intelligent really. It's just that ... that...'

'He isn't all there!' Felix broke in.

'Usually he's all right. He just has moments when he is a bit odd and ... rather frightening.'

'And yet you considered marrying him?'

'Well, Aunt Margaret and Uncle Simon were so insistent about it. They kept telling me how much Cyril loved me; that I was the only person who could help him. They pointed out, too, how much I owed to them.'

'It's the most fiendish thing I've ever heard,' Felix said. 'I'm not certain that they couldn't be sued for such behaviour. It is both mental cruelty and blackmail.'

'Oh, no, no!' Karina cried. 'You mustn't say that, Aunt Margaret has always been terribly kind to me in her own way. It's just that she's rather overbearing, and I don't think Uncle Simon can remember what it's like to be young. They love Cyril. I think to them he seems quite normal. They have always given him everything he wanted and ... and so, when he wanted me...'

'They were determined he should have you,' Felix finished for her. 'It's a pretty little story and if I hadn't turned up you would have walked up the aisle like a lamb to the slaughter, wouldn't you?'

'I ... suppose I should,' Karina admitted. 'It seems idiotic now. But before you came there didn't seem anything else for me to do.'

'Do you know how pretty you are?' Felix asked in a very different tone of voice.

She turned a startled little face towards him, her blue eyes wider than ever, her lips parted with astonishment.

'Pretty?' she queried.

'Lovely,' he answered. 'Oh, I know you haven't learnt all the tricks of how to make the best of yourself. But you look as if you are sixteen and have just woken up to look at the morning view. There are people who will find that far more attractive than any sophisticated London beauty.'

He paused and then added:

'And, of course, I am one of them.'

'Oh, Cousin Felix, you don't have to say such nice things to me,' Karina said.

'But I want to say them. You are a very lovely person, Karina; and when you have found your feet you are going to be a very beautiful one. Don't lose that look of dewy-eyed innocence. It will be the most valuable stock-in-trade you have ever possessed.'

'I don't know what you are talking about,' Karina laughed. 'Do you mean it will help me to get a job?'

Felix Mainwaring paused for a moment. He was going to make the kind of witty reply which would have brought a shriek of laughter from most of his friends. Instead he bit back the words.

'That is exactly what I do mean,' he said quietly. 'But we don't want to be in a hurry. We want to find the sort of job that will interest you, one at which you can make a success.'

'In the meantime I have got to live, haven't I?' Karina said with a flash of common sense, which seemed somehow at variance with the almost spiritual beauty of her face.

15

'You haven't got to worry about that for a moment,' Felix said.

'Cousin Felix, I can't take money from you – not much, at any rate,' Karina insisted. 'I have got a little of my own – three hundred pounds a year that my parents left me. Unfortunately I have spent rather a lot of it lately on … on clothes.'

'Your trousseau!' Felix said almost through gritted teeth. 'How they could dare suggest that you should marry that half-wit – and your cousin to boot – I cannot imagine.'

'We have talked about this before,' Karina said. 'Please, let's forget him. You promised me that I need never think about it all again.'

'Yes, I promised you that,' Felix agreed, 'and I mean it. I felt pretty sick at the whole idea when I first heard about it. When I found you crying in the greenhouse I knew something had got to be done, and pretty quick too.'

'You have been wonderful! Wonderful!' Karina breathed. 'But … but supposing they insist on my going back? If Aunt Margaret comes to see me, I shall never be able to say no.'

'She's not going to find you for some time,' Felix replied. 'You have got to trust me, Karina. And, having made you take this step, I shan't let you down. That is why you

16

are not going to look for a job right away.'

'What am I going to do?' Karina enquired.

'You are going to come and stay with some friends of mine,' Felix answered. There was a little pause and then he added: 'Have you ever heard of Garland Holt?'

There was something in his tone which told Karina that this was a name which should mean something to her. She racked her brains. Garland Holt? Garland Holt? She knew she ought to know who he was, but the name meant nothing at all. At the same time, she hated to disappoint Felix.

'I seem to have heard of him,' she said cautiously. 'Is he very important?'

'He's one of the biggest names in the City today,' Felix answered. 'One seldom opens a newspaper without seeing a report of him or his companies on the financial page. But obviously you are not interested in finance.'

'I'm not really,' Karina answered with a little smile. 'You see, I haven't so much money that I've had to worry about it.'

Felix's next question surprised her.

'Can you type?' he asked.

'Yes, I can,' Karina answered. 'And that is why I thought you could get me a job as a secretary. You see, Uncle Simon wanted his speeches typed out – the ones that he makes at the British Legion dinner, the County Council, and things like that – so Aunt Margaret suggested that I should help him.

'I hoped they would let me go to a proper secretarial college, but, of course, they wouldn't hear of it. Someone came to the house three days a week and gave me lessons. He was a nice old man, but it wasn't half so amusing as if I'd been allowed to go to a proper college.'

'They kept you pretty close, didn't they?' Felix said.

'I was allowed to go to school at a convent until I was seventeen. I loved being at St Anne's and I made lots of friends. I always imagined that I should be allowed to go and stay with them and perhaps they would come and stay with me. But then, at the beginning of the Christmas holidays, just before I was eighteen, Cyril began to ... to ... take an ... interest in me.'

Her voice trembled on the last words.

'What happened then?' Felix asked.

'Well, I think he must have told Aunt Margaret that he wanted to marry me. Anyway, I wasn't allowed to go back to school. I was told that I was out, that I was to be a débutante the following year. Aunt Margaret took me up to London and presented me the following May.'

Karina paused for a moment, and then in a very low voice she went on:

'I went to dances – quite a lot of them – but it wasn't much fun, because Cyril always came too and wanted to dance every

18

dance with me, and so I didn't get a chance to dance with many other people.'

'And you were ashamed of him, too. Go on, admit it,' Felix said almost roughly.

'Yes, yes, I was ashamed of him,' Karina said. 'That is why it didn't matter when we went home and Aunt Margaret didn't seem to want me to go anywhere.'

'"Why don't you play tennis here with Cyril?" she would say. Or, "Why don't you and Cyril watch the television?" Or, "...ride with Cyril?" Or, "...play cards with Cyril?" Everything that I suggested, the alternative was always to ... do things with C-Cyril.'

Karina's voice broke on the last word, and Felix put out a comforting hand and laid it on hers.

'Forget it,' he said. 'It is all over now.'

'I am only just beginning to realise how awful it was,' Karina said. 'It was like a nightmare that gets worse and worse and yet you know you cannot escape from it. I felt there was nothing I could do – and then you came!'

'Quite by chance,' he said. 'If my car hadn't broken down almost outside the door I had no intention of calling on my loving relations. I never could stick either of them.'

He gave a laugh which was mirthless.

'I remember how they asked me to some of those parties that you went to in London,' he went on. 'I don't think I even bothered to reply; just chucked the invitations in the wastepaper basket.'

'I wish you had come to them,' Karina breathed.

'I wish I had now,' he answered. 'But how was I to know that the child I remembered as rather a plain little thing had grown into one of the prettiest girls I have ever seen?'

'You'll turn my head,' Karina said with a little laugh that was both shy and uncertain.

'That is what I want to do,' he answered.

She was not quite certain what to make of this remark and they drove in silence for a little while. Then almost timidly she said:

'You haven't told me yet where we are going.'

'I am taking you to meet Garland Holt,' he said. 'His mother is a very old friend of mine. She has been very kind to me. I am going to throw myself on her mercy, and I have a feeling that she will be merciful.'

'But you can't force me on people who don't want me,' Karina said hastily.

'They will want you,' Felix assured her. 'All I want you to do is just to be yourself – natural, sweet, innocent and unassuming. For God's sake don't put on an act. I have seen so many women do that when Garland Holt is about.'

'What sort of act?' Karina asked curiously.

'Oh, showing off, being affected, ogling

him, if you like. When a man's as rich as Holt women behave like drunken moths round a candle flame.'

'Well, I'm certainly not interested in him or his money,' Karina said almost in terror.

Felix laughed.

'You haven't met him yet. You haven't realised how useful money can be. It's something everyone wants and few people can do without.'

'Well, I don't want Mr Holt's money, at any rate,' Karina said. 'All I want to do is to be able to earn my own living. If he can help me to find a job, I shall be grateful. I shan't have to stay with them long, shall I?'

'Just as long as they will have you,' Felix said sharply. And then, as if he remembered himself, he said in a very different tone of voice: 'Listen, Karina dear. You have got to trust me. I have got you out of that hole, haven't I? Well, just leave me to figure out what is the best thing for you to do. Don't go and try to do anything yourself until we've had a chance to talk it over. Is that a deal?'

'Of course I want to do what you say,' Karina said. 'At the same time, I don't want to force myself on anyone who doesn't want me.'

'You won't be doing that, I promise you,' Felix said. 'But I want you to do what I say is best. Promise me that you won't go round shouting that you want a job until I tell you to do so.'

'You are being very mysterious,' Karina said. 'Can't you explain things a little better?'

Felix Mainwaring did not answer for a moment or two, and then he said:

'We have only known each other for forty-eight hours. I shouldn't like to hurry you or frighten you, Karina, because you have had so little experience of the world. But I should like to feel that one day I was going to mean a great deal in your life.'

Karina turned her face swiftly towards him. He knew there was astonishment in those wide, blue eyes, but he did not turn his head from contemplation of the road ahead.

She studied his profile for a few seconds in silence. He was good looking, there was no doubt about that; and though he was only a second cousin, there was a vague family likeness to the photographs of her father which had stood on the mantelpiece in her bedroom ever since she was a child.

Cousin Felix! She had heard about him for as long as she could remember – heard disparaging remarks about his gaiety, the fact that he was always written up in the social papers, that he had a luxury flat in London and was seldom in it.

"Felix Mainwaring with the Duchess of

Downshire on the beach at the Lido."

"Felix Mainwaring at the Hunt Ball given in the Duke of Northwood's Castle."

"Felix Mainwaring in Nassau ... in New York ... at Cannes."

She could hear Aunt Margaret's voice saying distinctly as she held out the *Tatler* to Uncle Simon:

'Really, Felix is beginning to get quite bald on top. I suppose this dissolute life of his is beginning to tell at last.'

There had been almost malicious delight in Aunt Margaret's voice, and afterwards, out of curiosity, Karina had glanced at the paper. She had thought that the lady Felix was escorting to some gala was lovely – dark, mysterious and sophisticated; but Felix had appeared rather old.

Now, she looked at him in a startled manner. Could he have meant what she thought he meant? Of course, he wasn't really elderly. He couldn't be much more than thirty-five, and thirty-five wasn't really old.

'Well?'

She realised with a little start that Felix was awaiting her reply.

'I ... I don't understand what ... you are trying to say.'

'I think you do,' he answered. 'But it is too soon, isn't it? The only thing is, Garland Holt need not be afraid that you are yet

23

another woman who is running after him. I'm not taking you to his home just to lose you.'

'I … I want a job. I want to work,' Karina said.

'You shall,' Felix said soothingly. 'Don't upset yourself. Don't be frightened by what I have said to you. Just leave it at the back of your mind. One day perhaps we shall get to know each other a great deal better than we do at this moment.'

Without taking his eyes from the road he picked up her hand from her lap and raised it to his lips.

'Don't be frightened of me, Karina,' he said. 'You are trembling and it is quite unnecessary, I assure you. I am not a big bad wolf! Just Cousin Felix – cosy and kind who is going to look after you.'

His words soothed Karina, as they had been meant to do. She felt herself relax, and, leaning back, watched the road ahead.

It still seemed incredible that she had taken the step that she had and run away from Letchfield Park which had been her home ever since both her parents were killed in an aeroplane accident when she was only seven.

She could still remember her mother kissing her goodbye – the fragrance of her scent, the soft tickle of her furs which framed her happy face.

'We shall be back in a week, poppet,' she said. 'Daddy and I are going on another honeymoon. I will send you beautiful picture postcards of Rome and Florence and all the glorious places we go to. Look after her, Nanny.'

They were the last words Karina ever heard her mother say.

Then had come the move to Letchfield Park – the dark, big, sombre house which had seemed to close in upon her from the very first moment that she saw it. Her world had narrowed down to three people – Aunt Margaret, Uncle Simon and Cyril.

She felt a shudder run through her as she thought that if Cousin Felix had not walked unexpectedly into her life, she would, in five days' time, have been married to Cyril.

They had worn her down. She knew that now. They had not shouted at her or argued with her. They had not even appeared to coerce her, except by the insidious method of assuming that she wanted to make them happy, of reminding her indirectly a hundred times a day how kind they had been in taking a poor, unwanted orphan child into their home.

Night after night she had lain awake wondering how she could do it, hoping she would die before the wedding day came, knowing that every dawn brought her twenty-four hours nearer to it. Then,

Cousin Felix, arriving unexpectedly, had swept her off her feet. His disgust and horror at the idea of her being married to Cyril had been a far more persuasive argument than anything he might have said.

She knew then that was how other people would regard it – people from whom she had been isolated; people outside Letchfield Park; normal and ordinary men and women.

Impulsively she turned now towards the man who had saved her.

'Cousin Felix, I can never thank you enough for taking me away,' she said in her soft voice, which seemed to have some musical quality about it and yet, at the same time, was so young, so unspoilt that it seemed impossible that it should come from someone no longer in her teens. 'I don't think at this moment I could love anybody very much. I have been so unhappy and frightened for so long. But if you will wait...' She stopped, blushing at the intensity of her feelings.

'As I have already told you,' Felix said soothingly, 'I am prepared to wait until things right themselves, until we get to know each other very much better. It is rather exciting, don't you think, to start a new friendship with someone who attracts you very much but of whom you know so very little.'

He took his left hand from the driving wheel and laid it on hers.

'I want you to tell me all that you are thinking and feeling, about new places we are going to, about new people we are going to meet.'

'Supposing ... supposing they don't like me?' Karina asked anxiously.

Felix laughed.

'I cannot imagine anyone disliking you,' he said. 'Just take a look in that mirror you will find in the pocket beside you.'

Automatically Karina obeyed him. She pulled out the mirror with its grey suède back and held it up to her face.

'Is there anything wrong?' she asked. 'Have I got a smut on my nose?'

'Look at what you see there,' he said.

Obediently she stared at her face. The blue eyes were fringed with dark lashes – an inheritance from some Irish grandmother – a tiny, tip-tilted nose, a full, red mouth and soft, fair hair, almost ash blonde, waving against the pink and whiteness of her cheeks.

'I wish I looked older,' she said involuntarily.

'In which case you would not be here,' Felix said quickly.

She turned enquiring eyes towards him, and he added hastily, almost as if he had made a slip:

'I mean that if you looked older you would very likely be older, in which case you would have run away a long time ago.'

'Yes, I suppose I should,' Karina said. 'Oh, Cousin Felix, thank you so much! Thank you! Thank you!'

'I don't want to be thanked,' he replied, but she knew enough of men to know that he was pleased, and she made a mental reservation to go on thanking him.

They must have travelled for over an hour before they turned in at high ornamental gates and drove down a wide drive towards a huge stone house with a pillared portico.

'Are we there?' Karina asked nervously.

'We are,' Felix replied. 'Don't be afraid. I promise you everything is going to be all right.'

'If they don't want me, promise you will take me away,' Karina said. 'I can find a room in London while I look for a job? There must be something I can do.'

'Don't worry,' Felix admonished her. 'Leave everything to me.'

He drew the car up at the front door and, as the butler came hurrying out, said:

'Good evening, Travers! I'm afraid I am three days late.'

'You are, indeed, sir,' Travers replied. 'Her ladyship was very upset at your message that you had broken down. You weren't hurt in any way?'

'No, Travers. It was only a burst tyre. You will find my luggage and Miss Burke's in the boot.'

'Will the young lady be staying, sir?' Travers asked in a respectful voice.

'Yes, she will, Travers,' Felix Mainwaring answered.

He put his hand under Karina's arm and led her up the steps and into a great, cool hall. She had a quick impression of pillars and statues skilfully lit, of pale-green walls hung with pictures in gilt frames; and then Felix led her through another door, opened by a footman, and she found herself in what she knew was the drawing-room.

It was a big Georgian room with huge bow windows and a fireplace at the end, in front of which was seated a woman.

Karina had imagined Lady Holt to be old – why, she could not have said. But the woman who sprang to her feet with a little cry of welcome seemed incredibly young until one was very close to her.

'Felix!' she exclaimed. 'I had almost given you up for lost. Where have you been, you naughty boy? I have been worrying myself sick about you.'

'I was afraid of that, Julie,' he said, raising both her hands to his lips, one after the other.

'You are three days late! Isn't that like you!' Lady Holt said. 'And the Cartwrights couldn't wait. They have gone back to America, terribly disappointed not to see you.'

'I'm sorry about that too,' Felix smiled. 'But you know I would much rather find you here alone.'

Lady Holt took one hand from his eager grasp and turned towards Karina.

'Who is this?' she asked.

'My cousin,' Felix answered. 'My little cousin Karina Burke. And she is here, Julie, because she is desperately in need of help.'

'Really!' Lady Holt did not seem very pleased at the idea.

Felix drew her towards the sofa and sat down beside her.

'You have got to listen, Julie; and only you, in the kindness of your heart, will realise what this unfortunate child has been through. She has been brought up, since her father and mother – he was my first cousin – were killed in an aeroplane accident, by an uncle and aunt who have one mentally deficient son. Oh, he is not listed as that, nor have they acknowledged it. He looks fairly all right; but he is, in actual fact, not quite normal. His brain doesn't always synchronise with his body and he is at certain times of the month extremely queer.'

'It sounds horrible,' Lady Holt said a little petulantly.

'He is,' Felix agreed. 'And so you will

understand why I could not allow my cousin – though, indeed, I have not seen her since she was seven – to marry such a creature.'

'Marry? How could she have contemplated such a thing?' Lady Holt cried.

'She was being forced into it,' Felix explained. 'And that is why I have run away with her. We crept out as soon as it was dusk, threw her luggage into the car and came here to hide.'

Lady Holt gave a little cry and clasped her hands together.

'Felix, isn't that like you! So impulsive, so impetuous! I have always told you that it will get you into trouble one day.'

'And will you help me out of trouble?' Felix asked.

She smiled at him.

'I suppose so. Silly boy! I can refuse you nothing, can I?'

He kissed her hand again, and Karina, watching them, noticed for the first time that Lady Holt's hand was old, the fingers a little bent, the white veins showing. She looked more closely at the skilfully painted face; at the neck, with its six rows of huge pearls which hid the wrinkles; at the beautifully coiffeured hair, which she realised now must be dyed.

She had a sudden vision of Aunt Margaret with her grey hair drawn back into a neat roll at the base of her neck; of her face, lined, above her inevitable woollen twinset which did nothing to disguise the flatness of her figure. It was difficult to imagine two women who would be a greater contrast.

'Well, will you be kind to her, at least for a little while until we can find her a job?' Felix asked.

'But of course,' Lady Holt said. 'How could I refuse you, Felix? And how could I be so unkind as not to help this poor child?'

She put out her hand towards Karina.

'Come here, dear. You must tell me all about it,' she said. 'You are much too young to think of being married anyway, let alone to someone like that.'

'I am...' Karina began, eager to tell the truth about her age, only to catch a warning glance from Felix to silence her.

He obviously did not want Lady Holt to know how old she was and so she was silent.

'Of course you must stay,' Lady Holt was saying in her soft, purring voice. 'Tell Travers to prepare a room for her, Felix. I am afraid we have got a very quiet evening ahead. Garland may arrive about half-past seven; but he is not certain, and there is no one coming until tomorrow. Will you be bored?'

It was a question to which she obviously knew the answer, and Felix's garrulous compliments seemed to please her. She smiled at him flirtatiously over her shoulder before she moved across the room in a flutter of blue draperies to pour him a drink at the cocktail table.

Felix looked at Karina and winked. It was not a gesture she was expecting from him, and because it seemed so funny she gave a little gurgle of laughter.

The door opened suddenly and a man came into the room. But 'came' was not the right word. It was more as if he burst into the room – and yet actually he was moving quite slowly.

There was something so purposeful, so determined, about Garland Holt that he appeared to people who met him for the first time to almost have a volcanic quality.

Still laughing at Felix, Karina looked up at his entrance and met his eyes – dark, dynamic eyes which seemed almost, she thought, to bore their way though her.

'Garland! So you have made it!' Lady Holt exclaimed from the cocktail table. 'Well, that is splendid. And look who's arrived three days late.'

'Hello, Felix!'

Garland Holt held out his hand, but he did not sound as if he was particularly pleased to see Felix Mainwaring.

'Hello, Garland,' Felix said. 'This is my little cousin, Karina Burke.'

Garland Holt held out his hand. Karina put out hers. She felt the warmth and

33

strength of his fingers. She had the strangest feeling as if he were a magnet drawing her towards him. She felt as if he drew her – and then she remembered Felix's description, 'drunken moths round a candle flame'.

'Have I seen you before?'

His dark eyebrows were knit above his penetrating eyes. He would be good-looking, she thought, if he didn't appear so fierce, so uncompromising – the kind of man with whom you could never feel comfortable or relaxed.

'I … I don't think so,' she stammered in-voluntarily as she did when Uncle Simon barked at her for something she had done wrong.

'Of course you haven't seen her before,' Felix said. 'She's come to us out of the blue – it's a romantic story, if you care to hear it.'

'I was asking Miss Burke,' Garland Holt said. 'I suppose she can answer for herself.'

Karina looked bewildered. Why, she won-dered, was he so snubbing to Felix?

'I … I don't think we have met before,' she managed to say in a quiet voice, at the same time pulling her hand away from Garland Holt's grasp. It almost seemed as if he had forgotten that he was still shaking hands with her.

'Yes, we have,' he said. 'A ball in Belgrave Square three years ago. You were in a white dress and you went out on to the balcony when the dance was over.'

He paused. Karina's eyes were looking up into his as if mesmerised.

'You stood there for a moment,' Garland Holt went on, 'and you said, "I hate this! I want to go home!" That was you, wasn't it?'

'Yes, I did say that,' Karina said in a low, wondering voice.

CHAPTER TWO

Alone in her bedroom, where a maid had already unpacked her luggage and laid out an evening dress on the bed, Karina stood for a moment with her hands to her forehead. She was trying to think of all that had happened during the day.

It seemed impossible that only a few hours ago she had been at home in Letchfield Park and that even now her uncle and aunt would not have realised that she had left. It was unlikely that anyone would go to her room until she did not appear at dinner. Then they would find the note that she had left on her dressing-table.

She could imagine their amazed faces when they realised that she had run away. She could visualise their incredulity when they learnt that she did not intend to marry Cyril.

At the thought of him she shivered. Even now she could not believe that she had really escaped. She felt sure that they would find her and take her back, make her fulfil her promise, make her submit to Cyril's fumbling hands and the look of greed and lust that she had surprised so often in his small, shifty eyes.

How could she ever be grateful enough to her Cousin Felix? she asked herself. And yet, somehow, she could not feel the warm response towards him that she knew was his due. He had been so kind, so incredibly understanding. If he had not come to Letchfield Park at that very moment, if he had not found her alone in the greenhouse, she would never have been brave enough to run away, to shake herself free of the shackles with which they had kept her prisoner.

'He is so kind, so very kind,' she said aloud. And yet, unbidden, the thought came to her that she had only exchanged one gaoler for another.

She was appalled at her own ingratitude! Cousin Felix was going to find her a job. She would live in London on her own. She would work and be independent. Of course that was what was going to happen. Then she remembered Felix's words during their journey here, and the way he had hinted that they might mean more to each other than just friends and relations.

On an impulse Karina crossed the room, drew back one of the curtains and opened the window. Outside it was dark, and she felt the clean, fresh night air on her face.

'I am free!' she said aloud. 'Free! Free!'

But every nerve in her body yearned to fly

away into the darkness, leaving behind all the problems and difficulties and perplexities that had been hers for so long.

She didn't want to be held back. Above all else, she didn't want to belong to anyone. She just wanted to be herself, and she knew that she was afraid of Felix, just as in the past she had been afraid of Uncle Simon and Aunt Margaret and, most of all, of Cyril.

She tried to imagine what was behind Felix's motives in bringing her here. It was quite obvious even to the most unsophisticated eye that Lady Holt looked on him as her own property.

As she had talked to Felix before they came upstairs, Karina had noticed that her conversation was all about things they had done and things they were going to do – there was the picture Felix was having cleaned for her in London; a handbag that he had promised to collect next time he was in Bond Street; the play for which she had bought tickets because she knew it was the type he liked.

It was all so intimate; and yet, of course, Lady Holt was much older than Felix. Even as she thought this, Karina remembered that Felix was much older than herself. Did age matter in such things? She felt she was too inexperienced to know the answer to such a question.

She turned from the window and the darkness outside to look at the luxury of her bedroom. The fire was burning in the exquisite Regency fireplace surmounted by a Charles II mirror with a riot of gilt cupids and crowns. The carpet on the floor was so thick Karina felt as if her feet sank into it. The bedspread was of embroidered satin, while the curtains were of the heaviest and most expensive brocade. It all seemed to shout money, just as the luxury and comfort of the drawing-room downstairs had been the result of what unlimited money could buy.

Inevitably her mind came back to the man who owned all this – Garland Holt. She could feel his strange, dark eyes boring into hers. She could feel the almost electric quality of his handshake. And she remembered uncomfortably the scream of protest that his assertion that he had seen her before had evoked from Lady Holt.

'Three years ago! My dear Garland, it's impossible! The child would have been in the nursery!'

'I am never mistaken,' her son had replied. 'I remember it well.'

Karina, looking from her host to his mother, caught the expression on Felix's face and realised he was annoyed. She had somehow suspected that he wanted to pass her off as being younger than she was,

40

though why she could not tell.

'Anyway,' he said hastily, interrupting the exchange between mother and son, 'it is extraordinarily clever of Garland to remember such a tiny incident for so long. Of course, Karina was at that time only just out of school – a mere baby. You can hardly call her grown-up even now.'

'She certainly doesn't look it,' Lady Holt said.

Karina began to feel as if she was an inanimate object that had no thoughts and feelings; and then, before she could say anything, Garland Holt asked sharply:

'Did Felix bring you here?'

He asked the question of her, but he looked across her head to where Felix was standing by Lady Holt's side, and Karina knew that something antagonistic passed between the two men.

'I have thrown myself and this poor, homeless child on your mother's mercy,' Felix answered in a somewhat affected manner.

'Not for the first time,' Garland Holt said with a slight sneer at the corners of his mouth.

'This is different,' Felix replied briefly.

'I wonder,' Garland said.

Before anybody could make a reply, he looked at his wristwatch.

'I am going out for a breath of air.'

41

He gave a low whistle and two dogs which had been lying unnoticed in the far corner of the room sprang to their feet and came running to him. He turned away, walking down the long room and out through the door before, it seemed to Karina, anyone could think of anything else to say.

Then Felix turned to Lady Holt.

'Julie! If we are a nuisance...'

He didn't get a chance to complete the sentence.

'Don't be so ridiculous, Felix,' Lady Holt cried. 'You know Garland and how tiresome and disagreeable he always is. I tell him it is almost pathological that at his age he should dislike meeting new people – in fact it's quite absurd.'

'The last thing that Karina and I want is to be a bother to you,' Felix said in offended tones.

'You couldn't be a nuisance if you tried,' Lady Holt retorted, patting his arm affectionately. 'Pay no attention to that stupid son of mine. He may be clever when it comes to finance, but in dealing with human beings he is quite hopeless.'

Felix allowed himself to be mollified and coaxed back into a good humour. But Karina was left feeling uncomfortable and unwanted.

Why, she asked herself, couldn't Cousin Felix have done as she had suggested and taken her to London? He could have put her in some respectable hotel or boarding-house until she had time to find herself a room that she could afford.

She watched Lady Holt making a great play with her mascara-darkened eyelashes and pouting red mouth. Felix hardly opened his mouth without flattering her. She responded by making him realise how essential he was to her.

'Why does he do this?' Karina asked herself. 'It can't be for money.'

How could Cousin Felix, with his huge grey Bentley, expensively cut suits and monogrammed silk shirts, want anything from Lady Holt, however rich she might be?

It was a puzzle she could not understand, and at the moment she was too preoccupied with her own problems really to worry about Cousin Felix's. And yet, through no fault of her own, they were insolubly interlocked.

She walked about her bedroom now, restlessly, like an animal in a strange cage, until she realised that time was getting on and she must change for dinner. There was a bath drawn all ready in the bathroom adjoining her bedroom and, having bathed, she dressed quickly, putting on a short evening frock of white lace which made her look like a girl at her confirmation.

She was so small and tiny that she usually

found it easier to buy clothes in what was called 'the Junior Miss' departments at the stores; and as she could afford very few, she always chose those with the simplest lines in pale, clear colours which suited her white skin and fair hair.

She looked at herself in the long mirror and thought that it was understandable that everyone treated her as a rather stupid child. She did look absurdly young, and she made a mental note to buy herself a sophisticated black dress with the first money she earned.

A little shyly, because somehow she felt afraid of going back to face both Lady Holt and her son, she came out of her bedroom on to the landing and stood for the moment looking down the deep well of the stairs into the lighted hall below.

A voice behind her made her jump.

'You are very early,' a man's voice said.

She turned to see Garland Holt standing behind her. He was wearing a dinner jacket with a red cummerbund, and he looked larger and more frightening than he had done before.

'Yes,' she replied, conscious of how idiotic she sounded and wondering why he should have this curious effect on her.

He stood looking at her, taking in, it seemed to her, every hair on her head, every inch of her from her blue eyes, raised in

44

perplexity to his, to the toes of her white shoes.

It seemed to her that he was about to say something and then changed his mind.

'I'm going to see my grandmother,' he said abruptly in his rather ungracious tone, which somehow seemed antagonistic, however simple the words he used. 'Will you come with me?'

'Of course,' Karina answered politely. 'I should like to meet her.'

'She's a rather formidable person,' Garland Holt said, and he turned and led the way down the long corridor to where there were some big double doors at the far end.

He knocked and a nurse opened the door and smiled at the sight of him.

'Good evening, Mr Holt! Your grandmother was asking if you had forgotten about her.'

'Am I half a minute late?' Garland Holt enquired with a smile and he walked into the room, with Karina following behind him.

It was a large room and was dominated by a very large bed – a huge four-poster which faced the door, with a bow window at one side of it and a fireplace on the other. There were ostrich fronds in deep crimson touching the carved ceiling; there were long, red silk curtains falling from the canopy to the floor.

Sitting up in the bed, which was covered with an ermine rug yellow with age, was the most incredible old woman Karina had ever seen. She was very thin, her white hair was piled high on the top of her head and her wrinkled skin was like old parchment. Round her neck were twisted row upon row of fabulous pearls, and the thin, blue-veined hands which she held out to her grandson were loaded with rings.

'Here you are, Garland!' she said. 'I was wondering what had happened to you. You haven't got any time to spare for your old grandmother these days, I suppose.'

Her voice was sharp, at the same time deep, and her eyes, which were peculiarly like her grandson's, darted from his face towards Karina.

'And who is this?' she enquired.

Garland Holt bent to kiss his grandmother on the cheek.

'This is Karina Burke, Grannie.'

'Who is she? Another girl to run after you? I told you to keep away from them. They're no good to you, any of them.'

Karina felt the blood course suddenly into her cheeks, but Garland Holt only laughed.

'No, Grannie, Miss Burke is nothing to do with me,' he said. 'Felix Mainwaring brought her here.'

'Felix! Well, what's he doing with a young girl?' the old lady enquired. 'I thought he

46

had enough to do running after your mother, turning her head with his stupid compliments and making her load her face with paint until she looks like a circus clown.'

'Grannie, you're shocking Miss Burke,' Garland Holt said, with a note of laughter in his voice which he did not attempt to disguise.

The old lady held out her hand towards Karina.

'Come here, child. Let me have a look at you,' she commanded.

Karina did as she was told, fascinated by the dark eyes which seemed still youthful despite the wrinkles around them, and by the claw-like hand which was almost as cold as marble when it touched hers.

'Are you another of these harpies who are trying to trap my grandson?' was the next question that was asked of her.

Karina shook her head.

'No, indeed,' she said. 'My cousin brought me here because I've run away from home. I had never heard of your grandson until today.'

'Never heard of him?' The old lady seemed to take affront at this. 'Good gracious me! Where have you been living? Don't you read the papers? He's famous! Famous at twenty-nine! Everybody's heard of Garland Holt.'

'Everybody but one, Grannie,' Garland

Holt said. 'You see, I'm not such a success as you think.'

'So you had never heard of him,' the old lady said, looking at Karina. 'I wonder if that's the truth or another of your feminine tricks? We've seen them all, haven't we, Garland? The ones who have an accident at the gate and are terribly surprised to find whose house it is; the ones who wander into your bedroom at night, saying they want an aspirin because they've got a headache!'

The old lady gave a shriek of laughter at this and her grandson said reprovingly:

'Grannie, your bawdy talk is shocking Miss Burke.'

'She'll be lucky if nothing shocks her worse than that in her life,' his grandmother snapped. 'Now then, my dear, tell the truth. Why are you here?'

'My ... my Cousin Felix ... persuaded me to ... run away because ... because I was being forced to ... marry someone whom I ... didn't ... love.'

Even as she spoke the words in a low, hesitant voice, Karina thought how weak and stupid they sounded. Here was someone who had never been coerced into marriage. Here was someone strong and independent who must have stood up to the world and defied it even when she was very young.

'So you ran away?' The old lady said.

'Well, that was wise of you. It's what I'm always telling my grandson to do – to run away and keep running. But, still, you are a woman and a woman's better married. My grandson is different. If he wants to enjoy life, he's got to keep clear of all the traps those little vixen set for him.'

'Well, I've been very successful up to date, haven't I?' Garland Holt asked.

'Don't boast, boy, it's unlucky!' his grandmother snapped at him. Then, turning again to Karina, she said: 'Well, what do you intend to do now? You've run away from one prospective husband and you'll look for another, I suppose.'

'I've not the least wish to get married,' Karina said. 'My cousin has promised to find me a job in London and I want to start work as soon as possible.'

'Oh, you do, do you?' the old lady said. 'Well, if you take my advice you'll go back and marry this man who wants you. A chit with your face won't find it easy working in an office. What's more, you'll spoil that pretty complexion of yours and lose that innocent expression.'

She gave a harsh laugh.

'I know them, these girls who work. They all get hard-faced and hard-hearted. That's why they chase the first man they meet, so as to be able to give up their job and make him keep them for life.'

49

'Stop being cynical, Grannie,' Garland Holt said. 'You are frightening Miss Burke. Let her do what she wants to do. There's plenty of room in the world for everyone. They don't all have to live the way you live.'

'It's a pity they don't,' the old lady said. 'Your grandfather and I started the hard way – no money, no influence, only ambition and a determination to get what we wanted. We got it too!'

She chuckled.

'Worth two million when he died and when I married him he hadn't saved more than fifty pounds. That was an adventure if you like.'

She put her hand suddenly down on Karina's.

'Go back home, child. Marry the man who wants you and make something of him. There's nothing you can't do with a man if he loves you.'

'I can't do that – you don't understand,' Karina replied.

'Stop bullying the girl, Grannie,' Garland Holt commanded her. 'Can't you see she doesn't want to marry the man, whoever he may be?'

'And if you're not careful she'll be wanting to marry you,' the old lady retorted.

Garland Holt put back his head and laughed and Karina felt herself suddenly growing angry.

'I assure you,' she said, 'I have no intention of marrying anyone, and I think perhaps you overrate your grandson's powers of attraction.'

She didn't mean to be rude, but she suddenly felt incensed that this old lady, and apparently Garland himself, should be so sure that everyone was running after him.

The moment she had spoken she regretted it. She felt it was gauche and unattractive, and her eyes suddenly swam with tears because she had been so foolish. But once again the old lady only chuckled.

'So you've got a bit of spirit, have you?' she smiled. 'I like girls with spirit; it's what I've always had myself. No, I don't overrate Garland's powers of attraction. It isn't his *beaux yeux* they run after, it's his money, my dear. He's got the Midas touch, or so the papers call it. It's true, too. Now my son was no use when it came to finance. He lost nearly everything my husband had made – lost it by sheer incompetence. But Garland's made it all back, and more. That's why the girls find him so attractive. That's why they run after him.'

'Then I can promise you that I don't want money, whether it's your grandson's or anyone else's,' Karina said.

'Do you mean that?' the old lady asked, her shrewd old eyes searching Karina's face. 'I believe you do. Well, that's a change! I've never met a girl who wasn't after money, when it can mean jewels, furs, big cars, servants and comforts of every kind.'

'I don't want those things,' Karina replied. 'I just want to be on my own. I don't want people to order me about, to tell me to do this and to do that. I just want to live alone.'

'That's a surprise for you, Grannie, isn't it?' Garland Holt asked. 'You haven't got an answer to that one, have you?'

'Perhaps not,' his grandmother replied. 'But I shall think of one sooner or later.'

'We had better go down to dinner,' Garland Holt laughed, 'before you say anything else outrageous. Come along, Miss Burke. I'm afraid you will have to put up with a few people around you at dinner, for tonight at any rate.'

Karina turned away; she felt he was mocking her.

'I have been a fool,' she told herself. Why did she have to say what she felt or what she wanted? What did it matter to these people what was the real truth? A few conventional, polite sentences would have served her much better. Instead of which she felt as if she had exposed her innermost heart to their ridicule.

Outside in the passage she and Garland Holt walked along in silence until they reached the top of the stairs, and then he suddenly turned and smiled at her.

'What do you think of my grandmother?' he asked.

'I don't know what to think,' she answered.

'She eighty and, to my mind, utterly magnificent,' he said. 'She's got the strongest personality of anyone I know and a mind as keen as a rapier. I would rather have a word of praise from her than be made a Freeman of the City of London.'

'I suppose she's helped you in your career?' Karina asked a little cautiously.

'More than anyone else,' he replied. 'In fact, she is the one person who has helped me. Almost everything I have ever done is due to her.'

He spoke simply and without that aggressive tone in his voice which she had found so frightening and almost repulsive before. Once again he disconcerted her, for now she did not know what to say or how to accept his confidence.

Before she could reply they had reached the hall and the butler came forward to say something to Garland Holt, so that she walked on alone and in through the open door of the drawing-room.

Felix was standing by the fireplace with Lady Holt. He was holding both her hands in his and she was laughing at something he had said to her, throwing back her head with an exaggerated gesture as if she was an

53

untrammelled young girl instead of a middle-aged woman.

Karina had crossed half the room before they realised that she was near them, then Felix said, in his somewhat affected manner:

'Ah, here is my little cousin! I was beginning to be afraid that she had jumped out of the window and run away again.'

'I wouldn't do that without telling you,' Karina answered. 'Not when you have been so kind as to help me to escape in the first place.'

'I'm sure Felix makes an excellent nursemaid,' Lady Holt said, with a little edge on her voice. 'And it would be very stupid not to keep him pushing the pram until you have learned to walk on your own.'

'Julie, you're being beastly to me,' Felix said almost petulantly.

She capitulated immediately.

'I'm sorry, Felix. Was I being disagreeable then? I'll be sweet and nice, even though to look at this dewy-eyed child makes me feel depressed.'

'You are so ridiculously modest, Julie,' he replied in a low voice just as Garland Holt came into the room.

'Dinner is ready,' he said loudly from the doorway. 'Shall we go in?'

His mother looked across to him disapprovingly.

'Really, Garland, can't you wait for Travers

54

to announce it properly? You know how I hate these slipshod ways. It's so modern – and so unnecessary in this house.'

'I am sorry, Mother,' her son replied. 'Come on, Travers, do your piece; her ladyship is waiting to hear it.'

Quite unabashed by what was going on around him the butler, who was standing in the doorway, cleared his throat.

'Dinner is served, m'lady,' he said in quiet, impersonal tones.

Lady Holt moved forward.

'Shall I lead the way?' she said to Karina, and, not waiting for an answer, moved down the room, her short heavily embroidered dress rustling as she moved, the diamonds round her neck glittering and her long eyelashes fluttering as she flashed a smile at Felix.

They sat down in silence in the dining-room, which seemed to Karina too big, too pompous. The table with its silver ornaments, candelabra, bowls of orchids and dishes of fruit seemed almost overpowering for such a small party.

It appeared that the good humour which Garland had shown when he was with his grandmother had completely disappeared as soon as he was with his mother. He was morose, answering questions in mono-syllables and concentrating apparently upon eating.

Lady Holt talked almost exclusively to Felix, who held forth on every possible subject, appearing to Karina to be both charming and intelligent without being in the least dictatorial.

It was soon obvious to her, however, that Garland Holt thought differently. There was no mistaking the brooding look of dislike when he glanced at Felix or the note of rudeness in his voice when he occasionally contradicted something he said.

'How can Cousin Felix bear to come here?' Karina asked herself. 'He must see he is unwanted. He cannot be so thick-skinned as not to be aware that Garland Holt dislikes him.'

She had always been very sensitive to atmosphere. She always seemed to have an almost uncanny sense where other people where concerned, so that she would know what they were feeling however much they pretended or put on an act with the intention to deceive.

Now she felt shy and uncomfortable, while she listened to Lady Holt's high, gushing voice and Felix's low-toned responses.

'Tomorrow we have a large party arriving,' Julie Holt said. 'Bernstein is coming – you remember, the New York art dealer I was telling you about.'

'My dear, you won't want us if you have got a party,' Felix said. 'Karina and I will be on our way.'

'But of course not!' Lady Holt exclaimed. 'You know perfectly well, Felix, that I have planned this party especially for you. You wanted to meet Bernstein and he is coming. He is bringing his wife, which is rather a bore. I am told she is an incredibly dreary woman. But I have invited a lot of our friends, so perhaps she will be lost in the crowd and we shan't have to bother with her.'

'If you really want me...' Felix began, and Karina realised all too clearly that he had never intended to leave.

'I must get him alone,' she told herself. 'I must tell him that I must get away even if he wants to stay.'

It was so embarrassing to be an unwanted guest. But even as she thought this, Lady Holt gave a little scream.

'I have thought of something splendid,' she said. 'Karina will pair so well with Lord Monkham. You remember I was trying to find a girl for him, but really I had given it up as a bad job. They are all so tiresome or else preoccupied with other people. This makes the whole party complete. It was so clever of you, Felix, to bring her.'

Karina opened her mouth to expostulate that she could not stay any longer, and then caught Felix's eye. He was telling her to do nothing of the sort; to keep quiet; to leave

57

things as they were; and because she was so used to obeying other people she obeyed him.

The moment when she could have protested passed. Julie Holt was talking of other things; they were moving from the dining-room, the men coming with them because Garland Holt had said in his most uncompromising voice that he didn't drink port and that if Felix wanted any he could sit over it by himself.

'I hate the men being left behind,' Lady Holt said. 'It is an out-dated Victorian custom which should be swept away. Nothing is more dreary than being left to talk to the women about the difficulties of getting servants while you hear roars of laughter coming from the dining-room.'

They went into the drawing-room and almost immediately Garland said good night.

'I have got work to do, Mother,' he said.

'Of course, dear boy. But you work much too hard, you know that.'

She kissed him on the cheek, and Karina noticed that he made no response to kiss her back. It was very different from the way he had bent towards his grandmother.

The moment he had left the room she also got to her feet.

'Would you mind if I went to bed?' she asked. 'It has been rather a tiring day.'

'Of course, you poor child,' Lady Holt said. 'I only hope you will have a good night. Ring when you want your breakfast.'

'It is very k-kind of you to h-have me,' Karina stammered. 'I hope it is not a terrible nuisance my turning up out of the blue.'

'Of course it isn't,' Lady Holt said with a note of insincerity.

'I shall leave...' Karina began, only to be interrupted by Felix.

'Julie Holt is the kindest woman in the world,' he said. 'If you knew her as well as I do, Karina, you would know that everyone brings their lame dogs, ailing cats and runaway little cousins to find a haven by Julie's fireside.'

'But I only wanted to say...' Karina insisted. He touched her cheek with his hand, but it was almost a slap.

'Leave everything to your Cousin Felix,' he said. 'Don't worry your head about anything. You are free, no one knows where you are, and Cyril will be sobbing into his pillow. Run along, child, and don't forget to sleep well.'

Karina was dismissed. She knew it and she felt she could not fight to say the things she felt ought to be said.

She walked slowly up the stairs. The fire was blazing brightly in her bedroom and she sat down in front of it. There was so much she wanted to think about, so much she wanted to consider.

Felix, Lady Holt and Garland! They all seemed like figures on a stage, strange people encroaching on her life, altering and changing it. She did not know whether it was for better or for worse. She only knew that in some inexplicable way she was afraid of them all – especially of Garland.

CHAPTER THREE

The next day what seemed to Karina an enormous number of people arrived for the weekend. Most of them were businessmen with whom Garland was associated, but there were also young women, beautiful, sophisticated and exquisitely dressed, who made Karina feel gauche and shabby.

It appeared to her that Felix deliberately fostered the impression that she was an outsider, lonely and a little aloof from the others and therefore someone to pity. She could not explain even to herself how this atmosphere was created around her and yet she was sure it was so, and once again she felt that wild impulse to run away.

After luncheon, because she felt shy, she walked away from the crowd in the drawing-room trying to make up their minds how they would spend the afternoon. Moving down the corridors, she found herself, quite by chance, in a small room which seemed, even at first glance, quite different from the rest.

It was more austere and unluxurious, for one thing. At the same time there was something cosy about it – low comfortable armchairs; photographs scattered about the tables; a bookcase filled with volumes that were not there just for ornament but which had got shabby in use. There was a fire burning in the grate although the room was empty, and this did not surprise Karina, for she had already discovered that among the many luxuries in Garland Holt's house was a coal fire in every room whether it was being used or not.

She had been awakened by the housemaid drawing back the curtains over her windows and then laying the fire and relighting it before she carried in a delicious breakfast on a tray.

Karina now sat down in front of the fire in the small sitting-room and wondered who had used the room. She hadn't come to any conclusion when the door opened and Garland Holt came in. She looked up a little guiltily, wondering whether he had noticed her rudeness in slipping away from the party, at the same time questioning whether this was some private sanctuary of his own.

'I thought I saw you come in here,' he said.

'I am sorry,' Karina replied. 'Is it private?'

'No,' he answered, 'not at all. It is just a room that my guests seldom wish to visit. But for me it holds very poignant memories.'

She must have looked surprised, for he went on:

'You see, originally it was my schoolroom. I did my first lessons here; and when she grew old, my governess came back and stayed here until she died two years ago. This was her special room and I used to come and talk to her in the evenings. She was a rather wonderful person. Only after she died did we realise that she had been in agony for several years from an incurable cancer.'

'How awful!' Karina exclaimed.

'Not really,' he replied. 'I think Jetty was one of the happiest people I have ever known. She loved life, she loved people and she adored books. It didn't matter to her that she hadn't got any money. She could always find the three things which interested her most.'

'You sound as if you think money is what matters to most other people,' Karina said a little hastily.

'Well, doesn't it?' he asked with a note of sarcasm in his voice. 'Surely you're not going to pretend that you don't want money?'

'I want enough to live on, of course,' Karina said. 'Who doesn't?'

'It depends upon which standard you call "living",' he said.

She felt somehow he was deliberately being argumentative. With a pathetic little effort at dignity she said:

'I am sorry if I have intruded in this room. I expect you want to be alone.'

She rose to her feet, conscious all the time that he was watching her.

'You are rather overplaying your hand, aren't you?' he asked.

'I don't know what you mean,' she said wonderingly.

'The little lost-girl act,' he sneered. 'Try mixing with the others. You'll find it much more amusing.'

For a moment Karina stood quite still. She felt as if he had slapped her. Then with a flash of anger she could not control, she said:

'I think you are the one who should go back to your guests, Mr Holt. I did not ask for your company.'

For a moment he looked surprised and then he said:

'*Touchè!* And, incidentally, I apologise. It was gratuitously rude. As your host I have no right to be that, have I?'

She did not answer, but merely turned towards the door. And then, as she reached it, suddenly he was beside her, walking with her down the passage and saying in quite a different tone:

'You are angry with me. Do not be. I'm impossible – everyone tells me that, including my grandmother. What did you think of her, by the way? I asked you that before, but

I don't think you gave me an answer.'

Karina did not wish to speak to him, but she felt it would seem childish, so she replied stiffly, in what she hoped was a cold voice:

'I thought she was very interesting.'

'That's rather an understatement, isn't it?' Garland Holt asked. 'She's unique, original, a personality in a world that lacks character. My grandmother has lived a fantastic life. She's had three husbands, by the way, and buried them all. She made my grandfather successful against incredible, overwhelming odds. She married twice after he died, but I think she wore out her husbands; she was so full of vitality, energy and drive that they just couldn't stand up to her.'

There was an enthusiasm in Garland Holt's voice that had not been there before; and then, as they reached the hall where several guests were coming out of the drawing-room, he said in his more familiar, sarcastic, sneering tones:

'It's a pity they do not make women like that these days. If I could find a girl like my grandmother, then I should get married.'

'And if you did find one, I should think that it would be very unlikely that she would marry you!'

Karina was astounded to hear her own voice say the words and yet they came out of her lips almost without her conscious volition. And when she had said them, she was glad she had done so. She turned away from him and walked up the stairs.

'He's insufferable!' she told herself. 'Conceited and insufferable. How dare he think I am trying to attract his attention?'

She had almost reached the top of the staircase, hurrying towards her own room, when she heard her name called from behind her.

'Karina, where are you going?'

It was Cousin Felix's voice and she turned and saw him standing in the hall below.

'I'm going to my room,' Karina answered.

'Why? What for? It is raining far too hard for you to go out.'

'I wasn't thinking of going out,' Karina replied.

'Well, come down here. Don't leave us,' Felix said.

Although it was a request, Karina sensed there was almost a command in his voice. Then, as she hesitated, Garland Holt, who was standing where she left him, crossed to Felix's side.

'Persuade your cousin to join us,' he said. 'I expect she would like to see my jades.'

Felix turned to Garland Holt with an eagerness that had no pretence about it.

'I should like to see them too. Would that be possible? Your mother has told me so much about them, but I have never actually seen them.'

'I keep them locked up,' Garland Holt said stiffly.

'I have read about them, seen photographs of them and talked about them, but never, all the times I have been here, have I actually seen them.'

'Well, now is the moment,' Garland Holt said briefly.

Felix looked up to where Karina was still hanging over the banisters.

'Come along,' he said.

Reluctantly she retraced her steps. She wanted to tell Garland Holt that she did not wish to see his jades or anything else. 'He will only think I am envious of them,' she thought. 'He sneers at people who want money, but he is prepared to use his own to buy everything he wants.'

She had been too bemused last night to notice very much about the house, but now she was realising that almost everything in the way of furniture, pictures and *objets d'art* was worthy of a museum.

'It is all too rich,' she thought, and had a longing for a place of her own which would be small and simple, without the complications of a sneering young man who had too much money and thought that everyone was after it.

By the time she reached the hall Garland Holt had disappeared and members of the house party, who had been standing about in groups, had gone into the billiard-room to play snooker.

'How did you persuade him?' Felix asked in a low voice.

'Persuade him to do what?' Karina enquired.

'To show you his jade, of course.'

'I didn't persuade him,' she answered. 'I had never heard of it until this moment. What is it, anyway?'

'Good Lord! What ignorance!' Felix exclaimed. 'Haven't you ever heard of the Holt Collection?'

Karina shook her head. Felix began to talk rapidly.

'It was started by his father. He was a man of great artistic ability but no business ability. Garland, in some extraordinary way, seems to combine both. He is a wizard when it comes to finance. At the same time, he knows a great deal about pictures and, of course, this fabulous collection, which he has added to year by year.'

'Then why haven't you seen it before? I don't understand,' Karina said.

'It is too valuable to have lying about,' Felix answered. 'It has been in the bank for years, but Garland has had a special room made for it. It was only moved here a few months ago.'

Karina did not look particularly interested. She was angry with Garland Holt and she thought it a pity that he should think that by showing her something that he himself prized he could make up for being rude and disagreeable.

Felix glanced over his shoulder to make sure they were not overheard and then he said:

'You are doing splendidly. I saw him follow you down the passage.'

Karina stiffened.

'If you think I wanted him to...' she began angrily, only to hear Felix say quickly:

'Hush!'

Garland Holt was returning, walking towards them with something in his hand.

'Come along,' he said. 'I have got the key from the strongroom. All these precautions are a damned nuisance, but the insurance company insists on them.'

He did not wait for their comments but led the way across the hall to where, underneath the stairs, there was a door. He inserted the key in the lock. The door swung open and they found themselves in a small room almost completely square, in which the walls were covered with glass shelves cleverly lit.

On the shelves, iridescent in the light, were hundreds of pieces of carved jade. The effect was exquisite. Karina did not know enough about such things to realise how fabulously valuable and unique the collection was.

There was not only jade. There was pink quartz – whole shelves of it, each piece more beautifully carved than the last, the warm pink contrasting with other pieces of blue lapis lazuli, red amber and pure, transparent crystal.

She heard Felix gasping with excitement as he listened to Garland Holt describing a piece of burial jade or the value of a specially beautiful figure in red amber.

'I have never seen anything like it!' Felix exclaimed. 'And how wonderful they look here! You couldn't have chosen a better setting.'

'My father always had them in the bank,' Garland Holt answered. 'He would see them perhaps once or twice a year. I was determined to have them with me.'

'How often do you see them?' Felix asked.

'Very often,' Garland Holt replied. 'It rests me; and makes me feel relaxed to come in here and look at anything so beautiful.' He gave a little smile. 'Sometimes I think how long they have existed in the world – five, six, ten centuries – and realise that it doesn't matter one way or another if the deal I'm trying to put over today succeeds or fails.'

Karina glanced at him with a new interest. She hadn't heard him speak like this before. For once he wasn't being austere or aggressive, sarcastic or on his guard. He was just looking at the things he loved and enjoying the beauty of them.

'This is my favourite,' he said quietly and he took down from the centre position on one of the shelves a small figure made from pink quartz with emerald eyes.

Felix put out his hand, but Garland Holt gave it to Karina.

'What is it?' she asked.

'It is Indian,' he replied. 'It is Ganesa, the elephant god – the symbol of good luck.'

'It's so heavy!' she said in surprise.

She held it up to the light and saw the little stand on which it was seated was made of amethyst, set with diamonds.

'It's lovely!' she exclaimed.

'It must have been carved in about the thirteenth century,' Garland Holt said. 'And there is a legend that whoever possesses it will always have good luck. Originally it belonged to my grandfather. My grandmother always swears that his luck changed from the moment he was given it by a Maharajah whom he had befriended. Anyway, he kept it beside him until he died and then he left it to me – his only grandson – in his will. I have a feeling that it has brought me luck – any rate as far as money is concerned.'

'It is very beautiful,' Karina said. 'But if you lost it, would you be afraid?'

'That my luck had gone with it?' Garland

Holt questioned. 'Yes, perhaps I should. I tell myself that I am not suspicious, but where this is concerned it is almost a family heirloom. My grandmother believes in it firmly.'

'I think all these wonderful things have brought you luck,' Felix said. 'May I look at your elephant?'

He held out his hand and Karina gave it to him. She had a curious reluctance to do so. There was something in the smooth coolness of the carved stone which gave her a strange feeling, but what it was she could not formulate even to herself.

'It's fabulous!' Felix said. 'I shouldn't think there is a piece like it in the whole world.'

He placed his long fingers over the elephant's head, touched the little green emerald eyes, as if he was apprising every inch of it. Garland Holt suddenly bent forward and took it from him.

'Let me put my luck back where it belongs,' he said. 'I had a special lighting device where this was concerned. Do you see how it makes the eyes shine and shows up the transparency of the body?'

'Very clever,' Felix smiled. Then added: 'Have you any idea what this is worth? The whole collection, I mean.'

Garland Holt shrugged his shoulders.

'Can you put a price on things that could

never be replaced?' he asked. 'It is insured for two hundred thousand.'

'I hope you will keep it safe,' Felix said. 'There is no other way into this room except the two doors through which we have just come?'

'Not unless you break down the window,' Garland Holt said.

'The window?' Felix seemed surprised.

'The people who designed the room wished to keep it entirely artificially lit,' Garland Holt said. 'But I hate to dispense with sunshine when there is any and so I insisted on having a window.'

He drew back some curtains as he spoke and Karina saw that there was one long, narrow window between two sets of shelves which she had not noticed before. It was raining outside and therefore the light which percolated into the room was grey and sunless, but she could understand how, when the sun was shining, the light would pick out the exquisite colours of the quartz and jade.

'No bars?' she heard Felix ask.

'Ah! That's my secret,' Garland Holt replied. 'I wasn't going to have the place looking like a prison, so the whole window – which, incidentally, is very difficult to reach – has every sort of special burglar alarm that anyone has ever thought of. You have only got to touch a pane and the whole house will reverberate with the noise of a dozen bells.'

'I congratulate you,' Felix said. 'You seem to have thought of everything.'

'I hope so,' Garland Holt answered. 'I had enough people working on it.'

He drew the curtains over the window again and, walking to the door, switched out the lights behind the treasures. It was, Karina thought, as if he deliberately excluded them once again from the glimpses they had had of his true self.

'A lot of collectors would like to get their hands on this little lot,' he said in his ordinary tone, half jocular, half aggressive.

'I can believe it,' Felix said. 'Mind you keep the key safe.'

'Oh, I do,' Garland answered.

They stepped into the hall again.

'Well, that was certainly an experience,' Felix purred. 'I shall always remember that I have actually seen the Holt Collection.'

'And what did you think of it?' Garland Holt asked Karina.

'I think it is very beautiful,' she answered. 'But...'

She realised that she was about to criticise and stopped suddenly.

'But what?' Garland Holt asked.

She hesitated and then decided to tell him the truth.

'I think it is sad that anything so beautiful

should just be kept for one person,' she answered. 'So many people would like to enjoy the beauty that so many contrived.'

'I'm sure, Karina, that you don't mean anything so stupid,' Felix said sharply. 'The only way that Garland could let a lot of people see his jades would be to give them to a museum.'

'And why not?' Karina asked. 'At least they would be seen and admired rather than shut away in a dark room except when their owner condescends to visit them.'

She realised that what she was saying was annoying Felix. She saw the anger in his eyes, the sudden tightening of his rather thin lips. And then Garland Holt gave a laugh – a sharp laugh without any humour in it – and turned on his heel and walked away from them.

Felix watched them go and then turned to Karina.

'What do you think you're doing?' he asked.

'I ... I was only s-saying what I think,' Karina replied a little nervously.

'Then don't think such things,' he snapped. 'I want to talk to you.'

He looked round, then led the way to a room on the other side of the hall where there was a large, rather awe-inspiring library. The books, bound in beautifully tooled leather, were on shelves stretching

75

from floor to ceiling, and several big leather armchairs were arranged round a huge, carved stone fireplace.

Felix waited until Karina reached the hearth, then closed the door firmly behind him.

'Now listen to me, Karina,' he said.

Karina clasped her hands together.

'Please, Cousin Felix, don't be angry with me,' she pleaded. 'I daresay I have said the wrong thing, but Mr Holt was very rude to me. He inferred that I was running after him, trying to get at his money. He seems to think that everyone wants to get at him in some way or another. I think he is odious, conceited, spoilt and very unpleasant.'

She saw that her words were making Felix even angrier and she went on hastily:

'Please let us go away. Please let us go to London so that I can find a job.'

The room seemed to echo with her voice.

Felix did not answer her. Instead he stood with his hand on the mantelpiece looking down into the leaping flames, a strange expression on his face that she could not fathom.

She waited, feeling suddenly rather like a child who has been caught stealing the jam. The silence was far more frightening than if he had scolded her.

'Cousin Felix!' she whispered at length.

He looked up from the flames.

'I suppose,' he said slowly, 'that having made a mistake the best thing is to rectify it. You had better go back.'

She stood as if turned to stone.

'I thought you would be sensible,' he said. 'Obviously I was mistaken.'

'But, Cousin Felix! Please, what do you mean?'

The words were hardly above a whisper, but it was plain that he had heard them. His eyes, cold and with what seemed to her almost a look of dislike, looked her over, then turned away.

'I can arrange for you to return tomorrow,' he said.

'Back to Letchfield Park? Back to Aunt Margaret, to Uncle Simon and to ... to Cyril? Oh, Cousin Felix, you can't mean it!'

'What else can I do?' he enquired. 'You are obviously going out of your way to make yourself disagreeable to my friends, who have been kind enough to take you in simply out of friendship for me. I'm sorry, Karina, that you don't find them more congenial. But as it is, you force my hand to take the desperate measure of returning you from where you came.'

Tears started to Karina's eyes. She ran forward, her little hands outstretched, her face upturned to his.

'Cousin Felix! Please, Cousin Felix!' she cried. 'I didn't mean it. I swear I won't be rude again. I'll do anything you say, anything; only please don't send me back to Letchfield Park.'

Felix did not look at her.

'I should think it would be even unnecessary to send you,' he went on. 'A telephone call and doubtless your uncle would come and fetch you.'

'No! No! No!' Karina cried in sudden terror. 'You mustn't tell them where I am, you mustn't! I couldn't face it again. I couldn't go back. Please, Felix! Please!'

She was crying now, the tears running down her cheeks, her voice coming brokenly, racked with sobs, from between her lips. She put out her hand and clutched at Felix's arm.

'P-please, Cousin ... Felix, p-please. I ... I promise ... you I'll n-never do any ... thing wrong a-again.'

'What did Garland say to you?' Felix asked.

Desperately Karina tried to remember what had happened. It was difficult to think of anything but the terror that she might be sent back.

'I ... I went to the ... schoolroom and he ... came after me,' she said. 'He told me ... about his ... grandmother and his ... governess, and then he ... he seemed to think that ... that I had gone there ... deliberately so that he could ... come and be … alone with me. I … I'm afraid I was rather … rude to him, and then, when I tried to go upstairs to my bedroom to get away from … him, you called me and he offered to show us the jade.'

'He offered to show *you* the jade,' Felix corrected. He was silent for a moment and then he said, almost beneath his breath:

'I wonder! I wonder if this isn't a better approach!'

'Approach to what? Oh, Cousin Felix, you won't send me back, will you?'

Felix was silent for so long that Karina felt her heart drop lower and lower. The tears were still running down her cheeks and she made no attempt to stop them. And then at last, when she could see no more, she blindly groped for a handkerchief as Felix said:

'I'll not send you back, but you must not antagonise him too far.'

'Whom? Garland Holt?' Karina asked.

'Who else are we talking about?' Felix said irritably.

'But he is so … so rude,' she said.

'Millionaires are always rude,' Felix replied in a tired voice. 'And they're entitled to be. People will put up with anything if a man has a couple of million to his credit.'

He stroked his chin, looking down at her with an expression she could not fathom.

'Please, Cousin Felix,' she pleaded.

'He didn't show the jade to anyone else here,' he said. 'He didn't show the jade to... Well, never mind.'

'I don't understand what you are trying to say,' Karina said.

Felix sat down on the sofa.

'Listen to me, Karina,' he said. 'I'm beginning to think I have been wrong. At the same time, rudeness from someone who looks like you, and even repartee, is somehow out of place. Be gentle, sweet, at the same time retiring and a little lost. That is what one would expect.'

'But I am feeling ... lost, and I suppose you might say I am retiring ... because I don't fit in with the people who are here,' Karina answered. 'But why should you want me to pretend? What for? What is the reason?'

'I think you can leave that to me,' Felix said. 'Just do as you're told and don't be rude.'

'You won't send me back! Promise you won't send me back!' Karina begged.

'Not as long as you behave yourself,' Felix answered.

He smiled suddenly and, bending forward, kissed her on the cheek.

'I forgive you,' he said. 'You'd better go and bathe your eyes. You don't want anyone to think you have been crying.'

'I still don't understand,' she pleaded.

'Don't try,' Felix answered. 'Now, run along. I have a telephone call to make.'

Karina walked towards the door. There were a dozen questions she wanted to put to him, a hundred things she wanted clarifying in her mind. But she realised he had no intention of telling her anything more.

'Will you give me an outside line direct to this room?' she heard him say.

She stood for a moment hesitating in the doorway, hoping he would look at her, hoping that in some inexplicable manner he would make things clearer. But he was drawing with a pencil on the pad by the telephone, so she went from the library and shut the door behind her.

She ran across the hall, frightened that she would see someone. She reached the top of the stairs in safety and was just going into her room when a maid came down the passage and stopped her.

'Excuse me, miss, but Mrs de Winton said that if I saw you I was to ask you to come and see her.'

'Mrs de Winton?' Karina asked in surprise.

'Yes, the old lady – Mr Holt's grandmother. That's her name,' the maid explained.

'Of course,' Karina said.

She remembered that Garland Holt had told her that his grandmother had been married three times.

'I'll come in a few minutes. I just want to go to my room first.'

Karina went to her room, sponged her face with cold water and tried to hide the traces of tears with powder. She hoped Mrs de Winton would not notice. But as soon as she entered the old lady's room, her bright penetrating eyes scrutinised Karina's face and she said sharply:

'Who's been making you cry? Don't tell me it's that rascally grandson of mine.'

Karina felt that in truth Garland Holt was indirectly responsible for her tears, but she prevaricated by answering:

'How do you know I have been crying?'

'I've got eyes in my head, haven't I?' the old lady asked. 'And, what's more, I wasn't born yesterday. Something's upset you. What is it? Tell me.'

'My cousin was angry with me,' Karina said, 'and he threatened to send me back to Letchfield Park.'

'Oh! He's got a good hold over you if you're so frightened of what he might do that it makes you cry,' Mrs de Winton snorted. 'Take my advice, child. Never let anybody dictate to you. It makes you feel small and inferior, and that's bad enough without anything else.'

'I know, but it couldn't be helped,' Karina said.

Mrs de Winton looked as if she wanted to question her further, but instead she said:

'What's the party like downstairs? The usual collection of bloated financiers who eat and drink too much and take too little exercise?'

Karina laughed – she couldn't help it.

'They do look rather like that,' she confessed.

'What about the girls?' asked the old lady. 'My daughter-in-law told me she had asked the usual silly creatures who are always hoping that Garland will marry them.'

'He says he won't marry until he finds someone like you,' Karina said.

The old lady chuckled.

'So he said that, did he? Oh well! I didn't credit him with having so much good taste.'

She was obviously pleased with the compliment, and then she said with another of her penetrating glances:

'And why should you be discussing marriage with my grandson?'

'He brought the subject up,' Karina said. 'It seems to be something he thinks about frequently. He imagines everyone he meets is running after him.'

She couldn't help the scorn in her voice, and even as she spoke she realised it was the sort of thing that Felix did not want her to say. But Mrs de Winton was not annoyed.

'Well, they do, and that's a fact,' she said.

'When you've got a young man with money who has made a big name for himself, there are obviously dozens of silly young creatures who want to show him how to spend what he's earned. And think of how much publicity they would get out of being married to him!'

'You're as cynical as he is,' Karina said. 'I don't think that ordinary girls are like that at all. They want to fall in love and get married because they want to have a home of their own and children.'

'Is that what you want?' Mrs de Winton asked.

'Yes, that's what I should want,' Karina said almost defiantly, 'if I were going to get married. And I wouldn't want someone who had so much money that he was suspicious of every woman he met or who shut up all his lovely treasures behind locked doors so that only he could look at them. I think that would only complicate life and make it much too difficult.'

Once again she realised she was saying too much. Cousin Felix would be angry. She gave a little gasp and turned a scared face towards the old lady. But Mrs de Winton chuckled.

'That's the spirit,' she said. 'That's the way Garland ought to be talked to. You'll be good for him, I can quite see that.'

Karina felt a sudden panic sweep over her.

'You'll be good for him.' How often had she heard that expression before? Heard Aunt Margaret say: 'You'll be good for Cyril.' 'It will be good for Cyril to be married.' 'You must tell Cyril it will be good for him.'

She found herself suddenly clasping her hands together, clutching them so tightly that the knuckles showed white.

'I think I ought to make this very clear, Mrs de Winton,' she said. 'You may think it a strange thing for me to say, but I have got to say it. I wouldn't marry your grandson if he were the last man on earth.'

She heard the old lady chuckle again, and saw her eyes go towards the door. Karina turned her head sharply.

Garland Holt was standing in the doorway and must have heard everything she said!

CHAPTER FOUR

Karina could not sleep. She lay tossing and turning in the big, comfortable bed, finding it impossible to escape from the haunting remembrance of what had happened that afternoon.

Over and over again she could hear conversations repeating and re-repeating themselves and could see quite clearly the expression on the faces of those who spoke to her. She could feel, almost as if it were still happening, the sudden thump of her heart and the dryness of her mouth as she realised that Garland Holt was standing just inside the door of his grandmother's room, looking at her.

His eyebrows seemed to meet over his dark eyes. The very hair on his head seemed to be electric with the vibrations which appeared to pour from him, so that she was conscious of his anger and his indignation long before he spoke.

For a moment there was nothing but silence – a silence in which Karina felt that they must hear the banging of her heart and the quick intake of her breath. Then Mrs de Winton laughed, a high, cackling laugh which seemed, instead of easing it, to make the situation more tense.

'That's put you in your place, my boy,' she said with a chuckle.

Garland Holt advanced slowly into the room, walked to the bottom of his grandmother's bed and stood looking at Karina.

'I was not aware,' he said, and his voice was icy cold, 'that I had, in fact, asked you to marry me.'

Karina felt the tenseness which had held her almost paralysed since she had realised that he was there melt away. A flush came into her cheeks.

'I was not saying that you had,' she said, speaking so hastily that she tripped over her words. 'Your grandmother was just...'

The words trailed away. She somehow felt it was impossible to explain. She only knew that she hated him, as he stood there so strong, so tall, so overpowering, while she felt small, ineffectual and miserable.

Why had she been so silly as to speak her feelings aloud? Why had she let herself be drawn into expressing an opinion of any kind?

'Women are all the same,' Garland Holt said in an angry voice. 'They only think of two things – marriage and money. When they are not talking about one, they are scheming how to get the other. Money and marriage! Marriage and money! If there is a girl in the whole world who can think of anything else show her to me! That's all I ask, show her to me!'

His voice had risen as he was talking to Karina, and to her astonishment she realised that he had lost his temper. He turned to his grandmother.

'Why do I have to be plagued with all these people continually in the house?' he said. 'Can't you speak to Mother? Can't you persuade her that sometimes I want to be alone? You both told me that I had to live here. I wanted to be on my own. But surely I can have some privacy, some quiet, somewhere where I can work and talk to my own friends without this incessant feminine chitter-chatter.'

He was almost shouting by this time, but Mrs de Winton still only chuckled.

'You are using a bulldozer to squash a gnat,' she said. 'Can't you see the child's terrified – you great bully?'

'Terrified?' Garland Holt questioned, and looked at Karina.

The colour had ebbed away from her face and she was very pale. She had risen instinctively to her feet as he roared out his protest; and now, standing at the side of the bed with her hands linked together, she looked like a child who had, indeed, been badly frightened. Her eyes, wide and big, met his, and then she looked away towards

89

Mrs de Winton.

'I ... I must go,' she said in a voice which strove to be steady but yet trembled. 'I'm sorry. May I go?'

Mrs de Winton stretched out her hand with its glittering rings.

'Come here,' she said.

Obediently Karina went nearer to her and put her hand in hers.

'Listen, my dear,' the old lady said. 'If you are going to run away from everything that frightens you you will spend your life running. Stand up to things, face them, and you will find that most of your enemies are made of cardboard.'

She smiled and her eyes were kind.

'Take Garland, for instance. He's only a big blusterer. What can he do to you? Nothing! And he's only relieving his own feelings by shouting at us.'

Garland Holt gave a sudden laugh.

'I'm sorry, Grannie! I've made a fool of myself, haven't I? It's just that everything gets on my nerves.'

'Nerves at your age!' taunted his grandmother. 'You ought to be ashamed to say the word.'

'I know it sounds silly,' Garland Holt said with a rueful grin, 'but there have been some pretty complicated deals lately and I haven't been sleeping much.'

'I don't believe a word of it,' the old lady

said crisply. 'You've always slept the moment your head touched the pillow. So I don't believe any deal, however big, would keep you awake. Anyway, that's no excuse. You've frightened the child and that's all there is to it. You'd better make your peace with her.'

'Won't you intercede for me, Grannie?' Garland Holt asked with a smile which seemed to illuminate his whole face, making him unexpectedly handsome and in some extraordinary way appealing.

'That I will not,' Mrs de Winton said firmly. 'You've got to be man enough to do it for yourself.'

Garland Holt suddenly put out a hand across the bed towards Karina.

'What about it?' he asked. 'I'm sorry, I am really.'

'Please don't apologise,' Karina said in a low voice.

She realised that Mrs de Winton was still holding her left hand.

'You've got to forgive him, you know,' the old lady said gently.

'Have I?' Karina asked almost in a whisper.

'But of course,' Mrs de Winton replied with a smile. 'It's unlucky to refuse forgiveness when it is demanded of you. Hasn't anyone told you that? And as you are a woman, you will soon learn not only to forgive but to forget.'

'Then, of course, I ... I forgive y-you,' Karina stammered.

She didn't look at Garland Holt as she spoke, but she was conscious that his hand was still held out towards her. She still wanted to run away; she still wanted to evade both him and everything she could not understand. Yet it was impossible to do so. Not only was Mrs de Winton still holding on to her, but she felt as if she could not move. Her feet held her there.

With a reluctance that she could not even explain to herself, slowly, a little apprehensively, she laid her hand in Garland Holt's. His fingers closed over hers. She felt the strength of them. A kind of electricity came from him, almost as if she received an electric shock. She could feel the vitality of him tingling on her fingertips.

'I'm sorry,' he said again.

He was smiling and slowly and shyly she smiled in return.

'And now go away, both of you,' Mrs de Winton snapped abruptly. 'I am tired, and all this emotionalism is bad for me. Thank heaven I am past it. Now I just want to eat and sleep and forget what it is like to be torn in half by one's own feeling.'

'You enjoy every moment of living, Grannie, and well you know it,' Garland Holt said. 'You may be lying in bed, but I can feel you poking your finger into every hole and corner in the house.'

'If that's meant to be a compliment I don't take it as such,' Mrs de Winton barked at him. 'Run along, Garland, and take Karina with you.'

'I've got something to do in my room,' Karina said quickly.

He laughed across the bed at her.

'You heard what Grannie said?' he questioned. 'And she always has to be obeyed. No one has ever been able to refuse her anything. She's been a dictator since the age of fifteen. Isn't that so, Grannie?'

'If you mean by that that I always get what I want, you are much mistaken,' she replied. 'I want a lot for you that I haven't got yet.'

'Some day you must tell me about it,' Garland Holt said. 'Now you have at last said something which persuades me to run away. Come on, Karina. I must leave this room before Grannie decides I must climb the Himalayas, be the Prime Minister or the first man to reach the moon. Her ambitions are boundless where I am concerned.'

'It's all very well to have ambitions,' the old lady retorted. 'But one is always handicapped by the material upon which one has to work.'

Garland Holt gave a chuckle not unlike that of his grandmother's.

'Trust you to have the last word, Grannie,'

he said. 'Never mind, I'll surprise you one day. Then you'll be proud of me.'

There was no doubt that she was proud already, Karina thought, seeing the sudden look of tenderness in the old lady's eyes as they rested on her grandson. But she must have touched a bell by her bed, for a second later her nurse was in the room shooing them away and saying with professional firmness:

'Mrs de Winton must have a rest. I think she has talked for too long.'

Outside the bedroom door Garland looked down at Karina.

'I'm really sorry,' he said. 'It wasn't just because Grannie made me say so.'

'It's all right,' Karina said in an embarrassed tone. 'I shouldn't have said what I did.'

'Even though you meant it?' he questioned.

'Even though I meant it,' she replied. She hesitated a moment and then added: 'It is nothing to do with me, but why don't you live on your own if you find all these people get on your nerves?'

He hesitated as if he intended to answer her flippantly, and then, changing his mind, said seriously:

'There are several reasons, the first being that I think Grannie would die if I left here. She's very old, you know, but in me she lives her youth all over again. And it's true that she's ambitious for me. I always talk to her about my work, my deals, everything in which I am interested. It was what my grandfather did while he built up his fortune. She's got the quickest, most alert mind of anyone I know. I could never live alone while she's alive.'

Karina was surprised at the feeling in his voice. She didn't think he had it in him. And then in a very different tone he said:

'And then there is my mother. She's easily taken in by people – crooks, playboys and wasters. All sorts of riff-raff become her friends just because she's lonely and she likes people making a fuss of her. If I weren't here she would be bankrupt within a few weeks or else married to some fortune-hunter. So, you see, I have my uses!'

He spoke in his usual sarcastic, bitter manner. For once Karina was not disconcerted by it.

'No, you couldn't leave either of them,' she said quickly.

They had reached the top of the stairs. As they stood and looked down into the great marble hall below, they saw Lady Holt come through the door from the garden. She was carrying a huge bunch of carnations from the greenhouse, and behind her came Felix, a basket of daffodils and narcissi in his hand.

'You look enchanting!' they heard Felix say. 'Just like a picture that I used to love as a child, of Saint Elizabeth and the roses – only in your case the flowers are carnations.'

'I don't think, somehow, that I am a saint, Felix,' Lady Holt said with a little simper.

As she spoke, she passed through the drawing-room door and Felix's reply was lost. Karina felt suddenly embarrassed. 'Why must Lady Holt pretend to be so young?' she asked herself. 'That skittish, flirtatious way of hers must seem ridiculous to her son.'

Then Garland Holt spoke.

'What does that man Mainwaring mean to you?' he asked.

Karina's eyes widened.

'He is my cousin,' she replied.

'I know that,' he answered. 'But I thought there was something else. He hinted at some deeper attachment.'

Karina felt her face burn. So Cousin Felix had said to Garland Holt the same things that he had said to her.

'I don't know what he means by that,' she said. 'I haven't seen him for many years. He … he talked like that to me. B-but it means nothing to me. It is just that I am grateful that he helped me to escape.'

To her astonishment Garland Holt suddenly put his hands on both her shoulders and turned her round to face him.

'Listen, Karina!' he said. 'You are so young, so absurdly young and inexperienced. Do be careful what you do with your life. Don't say yes to everything that anyone asks you. Find what is right for you.'

'But how shall I know which is right?' she asked.

'Your heart will know it,' he said surprisingly.

He released her abruptly and then, without another word, turned and walked down the stairs, leaving her staring after him, the impact of his hands still heavy upon her shoulders.

'Your heart will know it!' 'Your heart will know it!'

Karina tossed and turned in her bed. What would her heart know? She had no idea.

After dinner, to her surprise, Cousin Felix had taken her by the arm and drawn her away from the drawing-room into the long picture gallery that ran the whole length of the house.

'Come and look at the pictures, Karina,' he said. 'You won't find better even in the National Gallery.'

'I'm so ignorant,' Karina said. 'There are so many things I have got to learn.'

'There's plenty of time,' Felix said. 'Plenty of time to learn all sorts of things.'

They walked down the gallery, but Felix was not looking at the pictures. Instead, when they reached nearly the end of it, he drew her towards a big sofa, and, sitting beside her, took her hand in his.

'I have been thinking about you all day,' he said.

'Have you?' Karina enquired.

'I'm always thinking about you,' Felix said. 'You are the sort of person, Karina, whom a man cannot forget. Perhaps it is because you are so small; perhaps it is because you are so trusting. There is a young, lost look about you which I find irresistible.'

Karina said nothing. She wondered where all this was leading. She wished, too, that Cousin Felix would not hold her hand. His own was rather hot. She thought perhaps it was because he had drunk so much champagne at dinner.

'Karina, I think you have brought me luck,' Felix said. 'In fact, you might almost be my mascot.'

'It sounds like something on a car,' Karina replied.

Felix laughed and squeezed her hand.

'My little mascot,' he said in a rather stupid voice.

'I wonder if things really can bring people luck,' Karina said quickly, feeling she must go on talking. 'I wonder if that lovely pink quartz elephant, for instance, is really lucky to whoever owns it?'

'That lovely pink quartz elephant, as you

98

call it, is famous,' Felix said. 'Of course it brings the owner luck. It always has, all through its history, all through the centuries, all down the years.'

'Well, I suppose Mr Holt is lucky,' Karina said doubtfully. 'But he doesn't seem to be very happy.'

'Lucky! When he's worth millions!' Felix said. 'You have seen some of his possessions; he has a great many more.'

'I don't think possessions make a person happy,' Karina said.

'I think that people often want what they think belongs to someone else,' Felix replied in what Karina thought was a rather crafty voice. 'Haven't you found that?'

Karina knit her brows together.

'No, I don't think so,' she said. 'You mean that someone would want the pink elephant just because Mr Holt had it?'

'I wasn't thinking about pink elephants,' Felix said. 'I was thinking of someone like you.'

'Like me!' Karina exclaimed in astonishment. 'But I don't belong to anybody – not now,' she added, remembering that if it hadn't been for Cousin Felix she would have been one day nearer her wedding to Cyril.

'And supposing I suggested that you belong to me?' Felix said. There was something in his face and eyes which put her on her guard.

With a swift unexpected movement she slipped her hand away from his and rose from the sofa.

'We must go back to the others,' she said. 'I think I hear Lady Holt calling for you.'

She had moved swiftly down the gallery before Felix had risen to his feet. She felt as if she were being chased, and only when she reached the door did she look back to see that Felix was not hurrying himself but was just standing by the sofa on which they had been sitting, looking after her. And then, as she opened the door, he laughed – a strange, amused and rather horrible laugh that seemed now, as she tossed in her bed, to echo and re-echo in her head.

'What is he trying to do?' she asked herself. 'He doesn't want me. Of course he doesn't want me. It is Lady Holt he likes – or is he after her money?'

It seemed absurd to contemplate, in spite of what Garland Holt had said about fortune hunters. Cousin Felix was rich, he knew everyone. There seemed no possible reason for him to attach himself to Lady Holt unless he was genuinely attracted to her.

And yet what had he meant by his conversation this evening? Why had there been that strange, almost fatuous look on his face? She could feel again the hot pressure of his fingers on hers, the close proximity of his body.

She shivered beneath the bedclothes, turned and tossed again. Garland Holt had warned her; he had told her that her heart would know the answer. And yet it seemed to her that there was, in fact, no answer to her questions.

She heard the clock strike three; and then, because she felt so restless, she went to the bathroom, sponged her face and drank a glass of cold water.

'I won't think about anything but going to sleep,' she told her reflection in the mirror over the basin. She didn't look sleepy. Her fair hair was a little tousled round her face, but her eyes were wide and bright, seeming to shine under the long, dark, curling eyelashes.

'It's because this house is too hot,' she thought. She had a sudden longing for the cool air outside, for the wind blowing across the fields, for the feel of the earth under her feet.

She decided suddenly that she would go for a walk. It was something she had often done at home when things had seemed unbearable in the house, when Cyril had been too attentive or Uncle Simon was annoyed with her. She had felt suffocated by rooms and walls and by the atmosphere of disapproval. She would go out, sometimes to saddle her horse and gallop until she was exhausted, at other times just to walk along

by the river or through the woods – anywhere so long as she could be away from
people, away from everything except the
comfort and kindliness of nature itself.

She knew then that she could stay in bed
no longer. Swiftly she dressed, putting on a
warm woollen coat and shirt and a knitted
jumper. She picked up a silk handkerchief
to tie over her hair and took her suède shoes
with their crêpe soles from the cupboard.

'I mustn't wake anybody,' she thought. 'I
will carry them in my hand and put them on
downstairs.'

She opened the door of her room quietly.
The landing was in darkness and she walked
across the thick carpet to the top of the
stairs. There were no lights; only a faint
lightness, which might have been moonlight, was coming through the high glass
windows of the hall.

As soon as her eyes were accustomed to
the darkness she could see the outline of the
banisters and feel her way without any difficulty down the stairs. She hurried down,
anxious now to be out in the air. The wind,
she thought, would blow all her troubles
away. Perhaps she would find in the rustle of
it amongst the branches of the tree the
answer to the questions which were per-
plexing her. Perhaps, more important than
all, she would know what she must do in the
future.

To go forward? To go back? Mrs de Winton had said she must face up to her problems. Would that achieve anything?

She reached the last stair and felt her foot strike the marble of the hall. It was then that she was conscious of a light coming through an open doorway a little to her left. She stared at it, wondering what it could be. Was there someone still in the drawing-room? She had heard what she thought was the last of the house party come to bed an hour after she herself had gone upstairs. Had anyone been left behind?

It was then that she realised it was not the door of the drawing-room through which the light was coming. It was another door, far to the left of it, and with a little leap of her heart she realised that it was the locked room into which Garland Holt had taken Cousin Felix and herself and which contained his fabulous collection of jade and quartz.

'He must be in there,' she thought, 'looking at his treasures, perhaps touching his lucky elephant.' It was the sort of thing she would do herself, she thought, to come down at night when there was no one about and sit with the things one loved, looking at them, realising with delight how beautiful they were.

She had already decided that she would not leave the house by the front door but by

the garden entrance which was a little way
down the passage towards the dining-room.
She would have to pass the door where
Garland Holt was looking at his treasures,
but she felt sure he would not hear her.

She tiptoed across the marble, her stock-
inged feet making no sound at all. And then,
as she neared the door of the lighted room,
she saw that the inner door was also open
and that there were two men there, not one.
They were bending over a bag which lay on
the floor and neither of them was Garland
Holt!

For a moment she could not take in what
she saw. Two men – and they were both of
them masked! Two men! And one of them
was holding a piece of jade in his hand and
the other held open the bag on the floor.

It was then she screamed. Screamed
loudly, her voice rising and echoing round
the hall.

'Help! Hel-!'

She screamed again and as she did so felt
something hit her on the head. The pain
shot through her, her cry stopped abruptly
as she staggered, tried desperately to hold
on to her consciousness, and then was lost
into a sudden darkness which seemed to
swallow her up completely and irrevoc-
ably...

She was travelling down a long, dark
tunnel, something was hurting her ... it was

her head... She could feel the pain of it seeping down over her whole body like the tentacles from an octopus, searing its way, aching with an almost unbearable agony...

She wanted to go back down the tunnel of darkness from which she had come... Suddenly she was aware that she was moving... It took her a second or so to realise that she was being carried, that people were talking in excited, almost hysterical voices... From above her head someone said sharply:

'Never mind the police. Get the doctor first.'

She heard the authority in the tone and knew who it was. Now she realised that he was carrying her. His arms were very strong and he was moving easily as if she weighed nothing at all.

She gave a little convulsive murmur, wanting to say that she could stand on her own, there was no need for him to carry her, but finding the words would not come.

'It's all right,' he said comfortingly. 'You are all right. Don't worry.'

There was something so soothing, so comforting in his tone that for a moment she obeyed him and let herself drift, giving up the effort of trying to remember. Then she felt him set her down on something soft and comfortable. For some unknown reason she did not wish him to leave her.

She tried to put out her hand, to cling to

him. She tried to ask him to go on holding her so that she would feel safe. But it was impossible to speak. She felt something warm being put over her legs, and now, at last, she managed to open her eyes.

A stab of pain in her head made her whimper. She saw Garland Holt looking at her, his face quite near to hers, and she felt his hands take hers, white and trembling, into his.

'It's all right,' he said again. 'The doctor will be here soon.'

'Some … body … hit … me,' she said.

'Yes, I know,' he answered. 'I heard you cry out.'

It was then she remembered the men with the bag, the man with the piece of jade in his hand.

'They were … burglars,' she said. 'They were taking your jade. They were burglars!'

'Yes, I know,' he said. 'And you disturbed them. If it hadn't been for you they would have got away with everything.'

'What did they take?' she asked.

'Quite a lot,' he said. 'But when you screamed, they got out as quickly as they could. But one of them must have hit you. I found you lying on the floor.'

'You found me?' she enquired.

'I heard you scream,' he said. 'I came running down the passage, but I wasn't in time to stop the men or see who they were.'

'I am ... glad I prevented ... them taking ... everything,' she said in an exhausted voice.

'You were very brave,' he said.

The door was suddenly burst open.

'What's happened? What's going on? They tell me Karina has been hurt.'

Karina closed her eyes. She felt somehow that she couldn't bear Cousin Felix fussing and asking questions. Her head ached terribly. Besides, his voice was loud and intrusive.

'There has been a burglary,' Garland Holt said briefly. 'Karina discovered them and screamed. I heard her and came downstairs to find that one of them had hit her on the head before they absconded with what they had already collected from my locked room.'

'Good heavens! Your jade!' Felix said. 'They haven't taken that?'

'Some of it,' Garland Holt replied. 'I really haven't had time to look. I was more concerned with Karina.'

'Of course, of course!' Felix said. 'My dear fellow, go at once and see what the damage is. I'll look after Karina.'

'There's no hurry,' Garland Holt said coolly. 'The doctor should be here soon. I told the servants to ring him up at once.'

'To think I should have slept through all this,' Felix said in a fussy, irritable voice.

'I'm a very light sleeper as a rule – in fact the voices downstairs woke me.'

'You didn't hear Karina scream?'

'No, I can't understand why I didn't,' Felix said, 'except of course, that I was very tired last night.'

'Well, it might have been worse,' Garland Holt said. 'She's got an enormous bump on her head.'

'I wonder what they hit her with?' Felix said. 'Why on earth, if Karina knew the burglars were there, didn't she come and tell me or you?'

He paused and then gave an exclamation.

'Good heavens! She's dressed! What does this mean?'

Karina wanted to explain, but really it was too much effort. Her head was hurting her, sending little waves of pain all down the sides of her temples. She felt a sudden warmth of gratitude as Garland Holt said:

'I expect she will tell us all about it when she feels better. Be a good fellow and go and see how much damage has been done downstairs and send the doctor up the moment he comes.'

'Of course, I'll go at once,' Felix said.

He went from the room, and Garland said in a quiet voice:

'Are you really unconscious or only pretending?'

'Pretending,' Karina answered, opening

her eyes. 'But my head does hurt so terribly.'

'I'm sure it does,' Garland Holt answered. 'Would you like me to send a maid to help you into bed or will you wait until the doctor has been?'

With an effort Karina looked to see that she was lying on a sofa in front of the fire. Garland Holt had covered her legs with the eiderdown from the bed and had propped her against a collection of satin and lace cushions which ornamented the sofa.

'I think I'll wait,' she said.

She felt as if it would be impossible for her ever to move again. Even to open her eyes sent little rivers of pain running through her body. The mere idea of moving her head was something too frightful to contemplate.

'I understand,' he said. 'To save you trouble, to save you being worried, would you tell me why you were dressed at three o'clock in the morning? The police will want to know.'

'The police!' Karina opened her eyes quickly. 'Will they want to know my name? Will it be in the papers?'

'I suppose there is every possibility of that,' Garland Holt said.

'It mustn't! Don't you understand? It mustn't!' Karina said. 'If Aunt Margaret and Uncle Simon know where I am they will take me back. I shall have to go home with them. I shall have to … marry Cyril.'

'You will have to do nothing of the sort,' Garland Holt answered.

'I shall! I shall!' Karina contradicted. 'Uncle Simon is my guardian and he will have the law on his side. Oh, please don't tell the police who I am.'

'I'm afraid they will insist upon knowing that,' Garland Holt said. 'But I will try and prevent your name getting into the papers. You must, however, tell me why you were downstairs.'

'I couldn't sleep,' Karina answered. 'I thought I would go for a walk.'

She saw Garland Holt smile.

'Such a simple explanation. I thought you must be running away.'

'That is what Cousin Felix will think,' she whispered. 'But I wasn't. I just wanted to get out of the house. It seemed to be closing in on me.'

'I know exactly what you mean,' Garland Holt said. 'Now, don't worry any more.'

'And you will keep my name out of the papers? Promise me,' Karina begged.

In her anxiety she reached out towards him, both her hands clinging to his, her cold little fingers seeming somehow desperate in their appeal.

'I'll do my best, I promise you,' Garland Holt told her, and somehow, quite unexpectedly, she felt reassured and comforted.

CHAPTER FIVE

The doctor gave Karina a sleeping draught and she slept almost the whole of the next day. When she did awake about tea-time she was interviewed by a very nice and rather apologetic Inspector of Police and the Chief Constable of the county.

She told them everything that had happened; but when they pressed her to say if she could identify the men again she had to admit that it would be quite impossible. She couldn't even remember if they were tall or short, fat or thin.

'I think it was the shock of seeing their masks,' she said. 'It was like a film or a play on television. I can only remember realising that they were burglars and were taking away Mr Holt's wonderful treasures of jade and quartz. I don't think I even thought about screaming. It just happened. And then something hit me on the head and I don't remember anything else.'

She knew they were disappointed with her, but there was nothing she could do about it; and after they had gone she found that her head ached so badly that she asked Mrs de Winton's nurse, who was looking after her, if she need see anyone else.

'You go to sleep and forget all about it,' the nurse said in the soothing voice one uses to an ailing child.

Karina was only too glad to do as she was told. She shut her eyes and opened them again only for a few brief minutes while she drank a little soup. Then she fell into a heavy dreamless sleep until the morning.

She awoke to find that, while her head was very sore and terribly tender when she touched it, the blinding headache which had made every movement an agony the day before had vanished. The nurse wouldn't hear of her getting up.

'Not until the doctor has seen you,' she said firmly.

And so Karina lay in bed feeling pampered and cosseted until the doctor came and said he was very pleased with her.

'You are a very brave girl,' he said. 'Everyone downstairs is singing your praises.'

'There is nothing in the papers?' Karina asked quickly.

'No, there isn't, and it's a pity,' he answered. 'It might have made you quite a national heroine. But, instead, they just said that the burglars were disturbed by a guest in the house. Another time take my advice and don't be so brave. Run to a place of safety and then scream.'

'I hope there won't be another time,'

Karina answered.

'So do I,' he replied. 'You're too small, too fragile for this sort of thing. A blow like that might have been fatal. As it is, you have had a lucky escape, young lady.'

'I will keep away from burglars in future,' Karina promised with a little smile.

While he was still talking to her there was a knock on the door and Felix came in.

'Is she better, doctor?' he asked anxiously. 'I was terrified yesterday. I looked in once or twice and she looked so pale I thought she must have died on us.'

Karina laughed.

'How ridiculous you are, Cousin Felix! I am much better and the doctor says I can get up.'

'Did I say that?' the doctor asked, raising his eyebrows. 'Well, for a couple of hours if you like, but not more. Is that a promise?'

'It's a promise,' Karina agreed.

'That's wonderful!' Felix exclaimed. 'I've been longing to see you and hear exactly what happened.'

The doctor said goodbye; and when Felix had seen him to the door he came back to stand beside Karina's bed. He looked so worried that she had to laugh at him.

'It's all right, Cousin Felix,' she said. 'I'm still alive, I am really.'

'If you had been badly injured,' he said, 'I should never have forgiven myself, never.'

'Well, it wasn't your fault,' Karina replied.

'No, but I brought you here,' he answered. 'I took you away from safety, if nothing else. I couldn't imagine there would be dangers of that sort lurking in this house.'

'What did they take?' Karina asked.

She had asked the same question of the nurse, but no one seemed to know.

'As a matter of fact I have just been checking the things with Julie,' Felix answered. 'Garland had to go up to London to see the insurance people and he asked his mother to go through the catalogue and see exactly what is missing. They got away with quite a lot.'

'Oh no!' Karina exclaimed. 'I had hoped I had saved all those lovely things for him.' She paused a moment and then she added: 'They didn't take the pink elephant, did they?'

Felix nodded.

'I'm afraid so.'

'But they can't have taken that!' Karina cried. 'It's his luck.'

'I don't think Garland is superstitious,' Felix smiled. 'Anyway, he doesn't seem to worry very much. If it were me, I should be frantic.'

Karina was silent for a moment and then she asked:

'Do you really believe that losing the elephant will affect him? That he will become unlucky because it has gone?'

Felix shrugged his shoulders.

'It seems ridiculous when you say it like that,' he answered, 'but the elephant has a whole history attached to it – people who swore their whole lives had altered because of it.'

He paused, then went on:

'It was originally owned by a Maharajah, and while he had it he was victorious over all his enemies. No one could stand up against him. And then it was stolen and from that moment his luck changed. He lost every battle, and finally he was killed.'

'Oh, don't tell me any more!' Karina cried. 'Poor Mr Holt. He must be worried even though he won't admit it.'

'They took most of the lapis lazuli and some of the burial jade,' Felix said. 'Those actually were the most valuable objects.'

'I don't mind about the burial jade,' Karina cried. 'It is the pink elephant that worries me.'

'That is a very feminine remark,' Felix said with a smile.

When Lady Holt came to see her later in the morning she, too, talked of her son's losses.

'Of course, Garland can buy more,' she said. 'But the collection was unique as it was. But, still, we ought not to complain. If it hadn't been for you, they might have taken the whole lot.'

'But how can they dispose of it?' Karina asked. 'Every piece must be known.'

'That is just the point the police made,' Lady Holt answered. 'But you see, dear, there are a great many collectors of valuable pieces of art who are prepared to buy anything unique just for the pleasure of owning it. They don't want people to know they possess such treasures. They just want to gloat over them by themselves.'

'You mean they arranged the burglary?' Karina asked.

'Oh no,' Lady Holt replied. 'They would do nothing. But the burglars must have been very superior types who know exactly where to place their stolen goods. That is why the police think we have very little hope of getting anything back.'

'I think it is disgraceful!' Karina cried hotly.

'So do I,' Lady Holt answered. 'But we must be grateful to you that they didn't take more.'

She rose to her feet and then said casually: 'Why exactly did you go downstairs at that particular hour – and dressed as well?'

'That is what the police asked me,' Karina said, 'and it sounds silly when I say it. But I wanted to go for a walk. I couldn't sleep and … well, I always have gone out at night.'

'I see,' Lady Holt said in a tone of voice

116

that told Karina she didn't understand in the slightest.

She was looking very elegant this morning in a beautifully cut coat and skirt of pale-blue wool. She wore an enormous brooch of blue sapphires on her lapel and a huge ring of the same gems glittered on her finger. Karina thought it was impossible to imagine Lady Holt so worried or beset by problems that she would lie awake restlessly, let alone want to walk off her troubles. She gave the impression of a hot-house flower which had never known the cold winds of poverty or adversity.

'Well, dear,' she said vaguely. 'It's a good thing that you did want to go for a walk, though I must say it seems a funny hour to choose.'

With a faint smile she went from the room, leaving behind her a fragrance of an expensive Parisian scent and the vague feeling in Karina's mind that her explanation was not satisfactory.

She understood this better later in the day when, having struggled to her feet, she came slowly downstairs to the drawing-room. It had been an effort to dress, and long before she was ready she regretted that she had bothered the doctor for permission to get up.

Anyway, having said both to Felix and Lady Holt that she would come down to tea, she felt it would look too much like weakness to send a message that she had changed her mind. So, feeling a little groggy and as if her head didn't really belong to her, she walked very slowly down the stairs, holding on to the banisters.

There was no one in the hall, and she guessed they were already all congregated in the drawing-room.

Tea was quite a ritual. There were huge silver trays, a big silver teapot and a kettle with a large methylated spirit lamp underneath it; cakes of all sorts and descriptions; sandwiches; scones; and big pats of Jersey butter to be augmented with home-made strawberry and raspberry jams.

Even the members of the house-party who swore they were slimming succumbed to the temptation of drop-scones just off the griddle and crumpets golden brown and buttery in a silver muffin dish.

As Karina crossed the hall she could hear the clatter of cups and the babble of voices. She felt shy and wished she had not come; and then, raising her little chin, she told herself she was being stupid. She had got to face them all some time and it need not be for long. The doctor had been very explicit that she must return to bed within two hours.

It was then, as she reached the door, that she heard what they were saying. One voice, loud and clear, with a slight drawl that she

118

recognised as belonging to Lady Carol Byng, said quite audibly:

'But you are all so stupid. Of course she let them in. Why else would she be lurking about the hall in her tweeds at three o'clock in the morning?'

Karina felt exactly as if someone had hit her over the head again. Because it was too late to retreat she could only go on walking down the whole length of the drawing-room, realising that everyone had stopped talking and turned to watch her come.

It was Felix who spoke first. He sprang up from his place on the sofa and came towards her.

'Karina, my dear! How lovely to see you! How do you feel? Is your head still aching?'

His words broke the spell and a little buzz of conversation started.

'Come and sit down by me,' Karina heard Lady Holt say, and she obeyed her, feeling as if her legs would hardly have carried her any farther.

'Now, what will you have to eat?' Felix said, fussing round the table. He brought her a plate and handed her sandwiches and scones, both of which she took automatically, conscious all the time of the blush on her cheeks and the burning indignation in her breast.

She did not look towards Lady Carol, but she knew that she was sprawling in a big armchair, a mocking smile on her lips, one long-fingered, white hand tossing back her heavy chestnut hair from her square forehead.

'Now, you are not to tire Karina with questions,' Lady Holt said. 'She's told the police everything she knows and really there is nothing more to say.'

'Everything?' Lady Carol asked with a mischievous and perhaps slightly spiteful lilt on her question.

'Of course she's told everything,' Felix answered for Karina. 'And everyone has said that if it hadn't been for Karina the burglars would have taken the lot.'

'But how did they get in? That's what I want to know,' Lady Carol said. 'The police told me themselves that it was an inside job. There was no question of breaking in through the window.'

'No, of course, we all know that,' Felix answered rather sharply. 'The inspector told me that it was quite obvious they had forced the lock of the garden door. They had then switched off the burglar alarm from inside the house and forced the other two locks. It wasn't very difficult. In fact I wonder Garland hadn't taken better precautions than that.'

'I thought it would all turn out to be my fault in the end,' Garland Holt said, and they all looked up and laughed.

He had not been in the room when Karina had entered, but he had come in a few minutes later and had stood listening to what Felix was saying. Karina had been aware of him the moment he appeared. It was not that she was looking in his direction. She had just known he was there; and now she looked up at him, remembering his kindness as he had carried her up the stairs and set her down on the sofa in her bedroom.

'Garland! When did you get back?' Lady Holt said. 'I didn't expect you until dinnertime.'

'What did the insurance people say?' someone asked. 'Are they going to pay up?'

Garland Holt walked into the circle round the table and, taking a sandwich off a plate, took a bite from it before he answered.

'They will pay in the end,' he said, answering the last question. 'But it is not going to be easy. They suspect me either of having burgled myself for the insurance money or all of you of putting a piece of jade in your pockets just for the devilment of it.'

'I hope you were firm with them, Garland,' Lady Holt said.

'I'm always firm, Mother,' he answered. 'May I have some tea?'

'Of course, dear boy. How stupid of me,' she replied.

Karina realised that the attention of the

house-party had been diverted from herself to Garland, and with a little sense of relief she felt herself relax. At the same time, she could not help hating Lady Carol for what she had said. How dared she think such a thing? How dared she suggest even for a moment that she would stoop to being in league with burglars and thieves?

'Is it true, Garland, that you lost your luck?' she heard Lady Carol ask now.

'My luck?' he questioned, helping himself to another sandwich.

'Your elephant,' Lady Carol said.

'Yes, it's gone,' Garland replied laconically.

There was a terrible cry round the table at this.

'But how terrible!' someone exclaimed. 'Aren't you frightened?'

'Of what?' Garland enquired.

'Well, that you will lose all your money, that the house will be set on fire, or that you will be involved in an accident?'

'No, I am not frightened of any of those things,' Garland Holt answered. 'I am not superstitious.'

'But I am,' his mother cried. 'I always have been. Felix and I turned our money last night when there was a new moon and we bowed seven times in the correct manner – and then this happens! But I suppose we can hardly count it as our bad luck. What do you think, Felix?'

'I think the real sufferer is Garland,' Felix answered.

'Yes, of course,' she replied quickly, as if she was glad that no vestige of bad luck could be attached to herself.

'What we were waiting to ask Miss Burke,' Lady Carol said, 'is why she was downstairs last night. It does seem such an odd time to go for a walk in the garden.'

'I think Miss Burke has already explained that quite satisfactorily,' Garland Holt said. 'She couldn't sleep and therefore she thought she would go out and get some air. There is nothing very peculiar about that, is there?'

'No, I suppose not,' Lady Carol drawled in a doubtful tone. 'At the same time, if she had left the garden door open it would have saved the burglars the trouble of forcing it, wouldn't it?'

'She was going out,' Garland said uncompromisingly. 'She was not coming in.'

Karina put her cup down on the table with a hand that trembled. She was not frightened, she was merely getting angry. Why should Lady Carol think such things about her? she wondered.

'Of course, that makes it all very clear,' Lady Carol said. 'Miss Burke comes downstairs, sees the burglars after they have already made a big haul, and then screams.

They hit her on the head – but not so hard that she is really hurt.'

She paused and looked round the room.

'It reminds me of what happened to June Cavendish,' she went on. 'Don't you remember? She found her maid tied up to the bedpost and all her jewellery gone. Then, of course, a few weeks later the maid disappeared too, and they found that she had been in league with the burglars all the time.'

Karina stood up suddenly. She was very pale, but her blue eyes were blazing in her white face.

'How dare you suggest that I was in league with the burglars the other night!' she said. 'You have no right to say such things when you cannot prove them.'

She tried to speak with the violence that was throbbing in her heart, her anger rising in her throat so that it almost seemed to choke her; but to her own horror her voice only sounded weak and ineffectual and the tears came rushing to her eyes.

'How ... dare you!' she stammered, and then to her dismay she realised that the room was going black; Lady Carol's smiling, scornful face seemed to swim in front of her. She turned to put her hand on the back of a chair, staggered, and then at that moment someone caught her up in his arms.

Even as the darkness swept over her,

Karina knew who was carrying her once again. She was only unconscious for a few seconds. When she opened her eyes, she was in the hall.

'I'm ... all ... right,' she said weakly. 'Put me ... down.'

'You little fool! What did you want to come down for?' Garland Holt asked.

She was surprised by the roughness in his voice.

'I'm all ... right, I can walk,' Karina murmured, but he paid no attention.

Once again he was carrying her upstairs, just as he carried her the other night. And suddenly she felt too weak to argue any further. It was so comforting to get away from the drawing-room, away from Lady Carol's accusing, quizzical eyes, away from Felix trying to make things better but merely making her feel embarrassed, away from all the crowd of Lady Holt's guests who, she felt, in their hearts all agreed with Lady Carol's accusations.

Garland Holt kicked open the door of her room and set her down on the bed.

'It was stupid of me to make a scene,' Karina apologised.

'I think you were justified,' he answered.

'She had said it before just as I came into the room,' Karina explained. 'It made me angry, but I suppose in a way it is what they would think. I'm the only stranger, the only outsider. All the others have known each other for a long time.'

'That is no excuse for what she said.' He thrust his hands deep into his pockets and walked across the room. 'It's damnable, but there is little you can do about it.'

'I think it would be best for me to go away,' Karina said. 'Could you ... could you suggest to Cousin Felix that he should take me to London soon?'

'What are you going to do when you get there?' Garland Holt asked. 'You can't stay alone in Mainwaring's flat, even though he is your cousin.'

'No, no, of course not,' Karina said. 'I want to get a job.'

'What sort of job?'

She made a little gesture of helplessness.

'I don't know,' she answered. 'Cousin Felix said he would find me something.'

As if his name had conjured him up, Felix came hurrying into the room with a decanter in his hand.

'Julie suggested that you should have a little brandy,' he said. 'I went and got the decanter from the dining-room.'

'It is very kind of you,' Karina told him, 'but I don't want any now.'

'Nonsense,' he answered. 'There's nothing like brandy when you feel faint.'

He poured some out into a glass on the bedside table and, putting it into Karen's

126

hand, said:

'Drink it.'

It seemed easier to obey him than to argue. She took a sip, felt it run down her throat and, because she was still feeling as if she might fade away, took another sip and yet another.

'That's better,' Felix said approvingly as the blood came back to her face.

The brandy gave Karina courage.

'Please, Cousin Felix, will you take me away? I can't stay here after what has happened.'

'My dear, I have got to find you a job first. You can't just trail about the streets of London hoping someone will employ you.'

'Yes, I know,' Karina said. 'But I thought you said you would find something for me.'

'I shall, of course, in time,' Felix replied, 'but it is not as easy as it sounds. You have no qualifications and no experience.'

Karina felt like crying. Was this the end to all her plans? If Cousin Felix couldn't get her a job, what was there left for her to do but to go home? Almost instinctively she looked towards Garland Holt.

'I don't quite see what you are making such heavy weather about, Mainwaring,' he said. 'There are plenty of jobs in London. We're always being told we've got full employment.'

'My dear Garland, there are jobs and

127

jobs!' Felix answered. 'Have you looked at Karina. Does she look the type of hardy young woman who could work in a factory or stand day after day selling behind a counter?'

'But I am strong, I am really,' Karina protested.

'And another thing,' Felix went on, as if she hadn't spoken, 'Karina, as you know, has got to keep out of sight for the next month or so. Coincidence is a very strange thing. It is always turning up when one least expects it. If she works in a shop, it is ten to one that someone will see her and will go and tell her aunt or uncle. They will be looking for her by this time, there's no doubt about it.'

Garland Holt stood in the middle of the room frowning.

'Haven't you got any suggestions?' he asked Felix.

'Not exactly, at the moment,' Felix said. 'I have been talking to your mother about it – you know how kind and sweet she is – and what she suggests is that Karina should stay here for a little while until I have had time to look round on her behalf.'

'I can't! You can see I can't!' Karina interrupted. 'Not after what Lady Carol said and ... and...'

'And what?' Garland Holt said unexpectedly.

'I ... I want to be independent,' Karina said. 'I want to stand on my own feet. Can't you understand? I have always had people making me do the things they wanted me to do. Just for once I want to be on my own and be my own master.'

'It is quite ridiculous!' Felix exclaimed. 'Absurd, when Lady Holt has been so kind. I can't think how you can be so ungrateful.'

'I don't think it is ridiculous at all,' Garland Holt snapped at him. 'Karina doesn't want to feel herself beholden to anyone.'

'Well, perhaps you can think of something for her to do,' Felix said with what Karina felt was a superior smile on his lips.

There was a moment's pause and then Garland said:

'Yes, I can. I will speak to Miss Weston. Karina can go with her. There's plenty to do in the office, and although Karina will be independent, she will at least not be able to get herself into trouble if Miss Weston is about.'

'Well, that certainly is a suggestion,' Felix said slowly. He rubbed his hands together and there was a grin of satisfaction in his eye which was quite unmistakable.

Quite suddenly Karina had the uncomfortable feeling that he had been scheming for this all along. The whole conversation had led up to this moment. He had deliberately been difficult and uncooperative. She even doubted if Lady Holt had actually given the invitation for her to stay on.

Because her instinct told her this was true, Karina wanted to refuse, to say no, that she would not work with Miss Weston, she would find something on her own even if it did mean working in a shop or turning a screw in a factory.

But it was too late. Felix had already accepted Garland Holt's offer.

'It would be extremely kind of you, Garland,' he said in his most ingratiating voice. 'It really would take a great weight off my mind. After all, Karina is not an ordinary sort of girl. She's lived a sheltered life and she looks so ridiculously young. I wouldn't have an easy night's sleep if I wasn't certain she had a decent job with decent people.'

'No one could accuse Miss Weston of being anything but decent,' Garland Holt replied with a faint smile.

'No, indeed,' Felix agreed. 'And if you ask me, I think Karina is extremely lucky to have the chance of working under her.'

He turned to Karina, who was lying very still on the bed, saying nothing.

'Thank Garland, my child. He's done you a very good turn.'

Karina parted her lips, but no sound would come. She didn't know why, but she felt this was wrong. Felix was manoeuvring something. She could almost feel him doing it. She and Garland Holt were being fitted like pieces of a jigsaw of which only he knew the pattern.

'I don't want any thanks,' Garland Holt said briskly. 'If you will take Karina to London tomorrow I will arrange everything with Miss Weston and Karina can come to the office on Wednesday morning.'

He walked out of the room as he finished speaking, shutting the door behind him with a sharp click. Felix rubbed his hands together again.

'Now you really have had a lucky break,' he exclaimed. 'You realise who Miss Weston is, don't you?'

Karina said nothing and he continued:

'She's Garland's private, confidential secretary, the woman who knows every one of his movements, everything he does. She's been with him for eight years – ever since he started to become a financial force. Everyone knows Miss Weston, she's quite a legend in the City. Some people say that she's the Svengali behind Garland – that he would never have got anywhere without her.'

He laughed.

'I expect that's untrue; but, anyway, as you are going to be with her, you will know all the big secrets which half the financial world would give their eyes and ears to know.'

There was a note of triumph and excitement in Felix's voice, and at last Karina was able to speak.

'Is this the job you meant me to get all along?' she asked.

'My goodness, no,' Felix replied. 'I didn't expect the whole works in one. But I don't mind telling you that I planned that Garland should take you into the office. Why not? Working for him will be far more interesting and far more lucrative than doing anything else. But to be with Miss Weston – well, that solves a great many problems with one stroke of the pen.'

Karina was not satisfied, but somehow she could not find words to express her feelings. Why had Cousin Felix wanted this so passionately? she wondered. Why did she feel embarrassed and even a little ashamed that he had schemed so cleverly and got what he wanted?

She didn't know the answer to this either. She only knew that she resented being made a pawn on Cousin Felix's chessboard. And yet, she chid herself, she was being ungrateful after all he had done for her.

With an effort she managed to force the words of thanks to her lips.

'You have been very kind, Cousin Felix. I must thank you.'

'I've been clever, haven't I?' he asked with a self-satisfied grin. 'I have got you away from an intolerable situation at home. I have found you a better job than any girl in your position could have imagined possible. Where do we go from here?'

'What do you mean?' Karina asked.

'Ah, that is something I shan't tell you,' he replied. 'I have other plans, deep-laid schemes, which will affect many things, but I am not going to tell you about them – not yet. In the meantime, keep on being grateful to me.'

He patted her on her shoulder and went from the room, highly pleased with himself. Alone, Karina got off the bed and walked across to the window.

Outside the February afternoon was dark and blustery. She felt somehow it reflected her own feelings.

'I should be feeling glad,' she told herself, 'glad that I can get away from here, glad that I have found a job.' But somehow the only thing that she could remember at that moment was that Felix had said she was to go on being thankful to him.

She had a feeling that one day he would ask her to repay the debt she owed him – to pay and to keep on paying!

CHAPTER SIX

Karina had never realised before that London was so big and overcrowded. She had come up from the country only once or twice a year with Aunt Margaret, either to buy clothes, to see a specialist or for some other sensible reason unconnected with either entertainment or work.

Then they had flashed through the streets in taxis, stayed at a quiet family hotel and had really very little contact with the overcrowded streets, the packed tube trains or the long queues waiting for buses.

She felt quite bruised and battered by the time she had fought her way on to a bus, travelled by tube and at last arrived at Garland Holt's office.

It was true that Felix had suggested sending her by car.

'I don't get up so early in the morning myself,' he said with a smile. 'But my valet will take you. He often drives the car for me.'

Karina had refused.

'I must begin as I mean to go on,' she said.

'You have certainly made a good beginning getting into Garland's office at all,'

135

Felix replied.

They were sitting in his flat having tea, having just arrived up from the country, and Felix was telephoning and trying to find her a room for the night in what he called 'a nice respectable hotel'.

'Tomorrow I will begin to look for a room,' Karina said.

'You won't have time,' Felix replied. 'Carter will find one for you. He's a genius at that sort of thing. He always knows where to put his hand on exactly what one requires, whatever it may be.'

The door opened and he raised his voice.

'I was talking about you, Carter. Do you think you could find Miss Burke lodgings which she can afford and which are neither dirty nor unsuitable for a young girl on her own?'

Carter put the sandwiches that he had just cut on the table.

'I'll have a word with my wife, sir. We might be able to accommodate Miss Burke ourselves now that my son has gone out to Canada.'

'The very thing, Carter!' Felix exclaimed. 'Karina, I believe that you have the luck of the devil – or should I say the luck of the pink elephant which Garland has lost. You will be very happy with Mrs Carter, and she is a wonderful cook. That's why Carter always looks so well and so young.'

'I shall have to ask the wife, sir,' Carter said, his expression remaining quite unchanged by Felix's flattery.

'Well, go and telephone her now,' Felix said. 'I wish I'd asked you before instead of wasting my time telephoning these tiresome hotels. They all of them seem to be full up with commercial travellers.'

'They would be at this time of the year, sir,' Carter answered, and moved from the room with the quiet, unhurried gait of a well-trained servant.

'He's a treasure,' Felix said to Karina. 'He has been with me now for seven years and I don't know what I should do without him. His wife comes and cooks when I have a dinner party. Otherwise I am seldom in for meals and Carter does everything that is necessary in the flat with the help of a woman who comes in the morning.'

'It is the most beautiful flat I have ever seen,' Karina said, looking round her.

She was not flattering her cousin but speaking the truth. She thought Garland Holt's house was fabulous, but there was only one word to describe Felix's home and that was – perfect. Untrained though she was, Karina could recognise good taste when she found it, and everything in Felix's flat was a glowing example of impeccable taste allied with plenty of money.

Every picture seemed to be worthy of the

National Gallery. Every piece of furniture might have graced a museum. But there was nothing ostentatious or vulgar about it. It was just the perfect setting for a man of culture and intelligence.

'I am glad you like it,' Felix said. 'I pride myself on being able to spot a bargain better than most people. That is why most of the things you see around you have been picked up for what the connoisseurs would call a mere song.'

'How clever you are,' Karina exclaimed.

He got up from his chair and came and sat beside her on the sofa.

'You are very sweet, Karina,' he said.

She repressed an impulse to edge away from him. He put out his hand and touched her hair.

'I wanted to see how you looked in my flat. I think it becomes you admirably.'

'Do you think it would be a good idea for me to go and meet Mrs Carter?' Karina said quickly. 'If she can't let me have the room, I shall have nowhere to sleep tonight.'

'I will find you somewhere,' Felix said reassuringly. 'It's a pity you can't stay here.'

'Yes, isn't it?' Karina answered.

She wished Felix would not put his face so near to hers. She also found herself disliking the way he was smoothing her hair with his fingers.

'You are pretty, very pretty,' Felix said in

that soft voice which made her somehow afraid. 'You won't forget to be grateful to me for all this, will you, my dear?'

'I am grateful, you know I am,' Karina said. 'And one day I hope to repay you.'

'And what will you give me?' Felix asked in an amused voice. 'A half of your kingdom? Or shall it be your hand in marriage?'

Karina moved away from him and with a lithe movement of her body managed to rise to her feet.

'I want to look round,' she said. 'I want to look at your pictures and that lovely china over there.'

'I think you are running away from me,' Felix accused. 'One day, Karina, you will have to stop running and face up to things.'

'But that day has not come yet,' Karina retorted.

'No, not yet,' he replied with a smile on his lips. 'But when it does…'

She found herself standing waiting for him to complete his sentence. But what he was about to say was never completed because Carter came into the room.

'I have spoken to my wife, sir.'

'Yes, Carter, and what does she say?'

'She says she will be delighted to have the young lady.'

'That's splendid, Carter,' Felix exclaimed.

'Perhaps, if I might make a suggestion, sir, I will take Miss Burke round myself. I shall then be able to carry her suitcase up to her bedroom.'

'Yes, of course,' Felix agreed. 'It won't take you long, and then you can bring her back and I will take Miss Burke out to dinner.'

Karina parted her lips to say that perhaps it would be better for her to stay in tonight, then changed her mind. Cousin Felix had been kind, so kind to her that it would be gross ingratitude not to do what he wished. At the same time, she wished she didn't feel so unsure of herself when she was with him. He had the effect of making her feel embarrassed, afraid and also gauche and stupid.

She wished she was sophisticated and experienced like the girls who had been staying with Lady Holt, who had laughed at Felix and teased him. But where she was concerned every word he uttered seemed to be fraught with some hidden meaning.

But now, as she stepped out of the tube station on to a wet and rainy pavement, she thought how very different her life was going to be from Felix's or from the girls' with whom he seemed on such easy, equal terms. She was going to work, and she promised herself that she was going to make a success of it.

She put up her umbrella and hurried down the street. She stopped a policeman and he told her that the block of offices she was seeking was down the second turning on the left. She hurried on again.

It was fun last night, she thought as she went. She had enjoyed it because it was all so strange and exciting to be dining in a restaurant, to be dancing to a band rather than just hearing the tunes playing on the wireless or on the old gramophone she had in her room at Letchfield Park. But what she had not liked was being clasped so tightly in Cousin Felix's arms.

'We are going to have fun together,' he told her. 'Lots of fun. I'll show you London. I'll show you lots of other things too. It's rather exciting to have such an innocent, inexperienced little cousin.'

'I mustn't stay up late at night if I'm working early in the morning,' Karina said.

'We shall have to make Garland forgive you if you are late,' Felix said jokingly.

Karina shook her head.

'I think Mr Holt is the sort of person who would always put business in front of pleasure,' she said. 'I don't think he would understand anyone doing anything else.'

'You judge him very shrewdly,' Felix smiled. 'What did he say to you when he carried you upstairs the other afternoon?'

'Nothing,' Karina answered quickly. 'It was stupid of me to make a scene. I should have taken no notice.'

'I have never known Garland so attentive,'

Felix said. 'So long as he doesn't think you are running after him he will be interested in you. It is well known that as soon as a woman looks at him with love in her eyes he runs from her.'

'I am not thinking of looking at him with love in my eyes,' Karina said stiffly.

'No, of course you're not,' Felix agreed. 'And if he does question you about what you are doing in London, tell him you are enjoying yourself with me, tell him we are going everywhere together – because it's true, isn't it?'

He put his hands over hers and there was something possessive about him which made Karina pick up her wrap and put it round her shoulders.

'I think we ought to go home,' she said. 'I have got to be up early in the morning.'

She was half afraid that Felix might try to kiss her when they were driving back, but he made no attempt to touch her. Only when they reached the house where Mr and Mrs Carter lived, in a narrow street near Paddington Station, did he say:

'Don't forget, Karina. Tell Garland that you are my girl.'

'He's not likely to ask me,' Karina replied quickly. 'And, anyway, it isn't true, Cousin Felix. I don't belong to anyone.'

She jumped out of the car before he could reply and by the time he had got out on his side she had already taken her latchkey out of her bag and was fitting it into the lock.

'Thank you so much for taking me out,' she said. 'Good night, Cousin Felix.'

The door was open and she was slipping through it as he took hold of her hand.

'Good night, my most elusive and adorable little cousin.'

He bent his head and kissed her fingers and then, turning her hand over, kissed the palm. She felt as if his lips burned against her skin, and then the door was shut behind her and she was running upstairs as quickly as she could.

In her small but spotlessly clean bedroom she shut the door and locked it, conscious that her breath was coming quickly and her heart pounding with fear.

'Why does he have this effect on me?' she asked herself.

She asked it again now as she turned down the street to which the policeman had directed her. The offices were in a new block, and after staring at the names in the hall she found Garland Holt's written against the eighth floor.

The lift carried her up. Now she began to feel more apprehensive about what lay ahead than worried about what was already in the past. It seemed to her that hundreds of people were working in the big office into which she walked, feeling very small and very insignificant. And then, as her shyness evaporated a little, she saw there were about a dozen girls and two men, all sitting at big desks, most of them typing or engaged in speaking on the telephone.

'Can I help you?'

It was a rather pretty, dark-haired girl in a red sweater who asked the question.

'I have been told to ask for Miss Weston,' Karina said.

'Oh, you're Miss Burke, aren't you?' the girl smiled. 'I was told to expect you. Will you come this way?'

She led the way across the office, and Karina was conscious that most of the people working there turned their heads to watch her pass.

'I hope I'm not late,' Karina said nervously.

'Oh no,' the girl answered. 'Miss Weston doesn't get here until a quarter-past nine, but we have to be here at nine. She should be arriving at any moment now.'

She took Karina into a smaller room where there were two desks and the windows were shaded by Venetian blinds.

'Miss Weston will not be long,' the dark girl said. 'By the way, my name is Beth.'

'And I'm Karina.'

They shook hands solemnly.

'Is this your first job?' Beth enquired.

Karina nodded.

'I'm very nervous.'

'Oh, don't worry,' Beth replied. 'There are plenty of other places wanting typists. In fact we are increasingly in demand. In consequence people are much nicer than they used to be when I first came into the City.'

'You don't look as if you're old enough to have been working long,' Karina said.

'Five years – I'm twenty-one,' Beth answered. 'And pretty hardened by this time. Don't worry, I'll show you the ropes. And Miss Weston isn't a bad old thing really.'

'Thank you,' Karina said.

She somehow felt warmed by Beth's friendliness; and when a few seconds later Miss Weston came into the room she was not so nervous as she might have been.

She had expected someone old, austere and terrifying. But to her surprise she found herself looking at a very attractive smartly dressed woman of about forty-five who didn't seem in the least the dragon she had been led to expect.

'How do you do, Miss Burke. Mr Holt has told me about you. I hope you are going to like working for us.'

Miss Weston's voice was low and musical. Karina was to learn later that this was one of her most important assets. People in the City not only referred to her as 'the golden-voiced secretary', but also found that she could charm them out of their most disagreeable moods and put them in a good temper long before Garland Holt spoke to them.

'I am afraid you will find this all very strange to begin with,' Miss Weston went on. 'But Mr Holt has asked me to look after you myself and so I have arranged for you to be in this room with me.'

'I hope I shan't be too much of a nuisance,' Karina said.

'I am sure you won't,' Miss Weston replied. 'There are quite a lot of things you can do, for instance, which will help me. We'll start off with some typing. There are some letters here which have got to be copied. If you could get on with these, it will give us both time to find our breath and discover what comes next.'

Karina was typing busily when, twenty minutes later, Garland Holt came striding through the room and out through another door on the other side which she had already learned was his special sanctum. Obviously something had gone wrong, for he was at his most formidable.

He walked past with his brows knit together, calling to Miss Weston to follow him, and the door slammed behind them both, Karina could not hear what was said in the inner office. But she could hear the telephone ringing and once or twice during the next hour, Miss Weston came out, called one of the girls from outside, gave her a mass of instructions and disappeared inside again.

And then as abruptly as he had arrived, Garland Holt was gone. He strode out, giving last-minute orders as he went.

'Ring up Wembury's and if they can't do it get on to Harley and Black. Tell Tomlinson to telephone at five o'clock and let me know the prices. And by the way' – he was almost through the outer office by this time –'tell Sir Charles I can't lunch with him to-morrow.'

Miss Weston, frantically scribbling in her notebook, was following behind him.

'Very good, Mr Holt,' she said. 'And what about Levinsons?'

'Thank heaven you remembered them!' Karina heard Garland Holt say. 'Stave them off for the moment. Make any excuse you like but leave the door open.'

He was gone, and Karina could almost hear the sigh of relief that went up. Miss Weston came back to her desk and started telephoning. What she did seemed very incomprehensible to Karina, but she couldn't help but note how charmingly she gave all the messages.

'Mr Holt is so sorry to inconvenience you. He feels sure you will understand...' she

147

would begin. Or, 'Mr Holt thanks you so much for your kind letter. It was just what he wanted to know...'

Karina smiled to herself, remembering Garland Holt's staccato instructions and thinking that if they had been given in that manner they would have received a very different reception.

They were both still busy, Karina with the humble job of copying a letter which had already been typed, when a young man came into the office. He was good-looking, dark and extremely well dressed in a blue suit with a white stripe and wearing a red carnation in his buttonhole. He was carrying a bowler hat and a tightly rolled umbrella.

'Hallo, Westie!' he said. 'Is the great man in?'

'No, Mr Jim, he isn't,' she replied. 'And I'll thank you not to call me Westie.'

'Where's he gone?' the newcomer asked. 'I was wondering if I could sell him a new car.'

Miss Weston put down the telephone.

'Mr Jim, you haven't lost that other job?'

'Which one?'

'The one with the stockbrokers. Mr Holt went to so much trouble to get it for you.'

The young man sat down on the edge of the desk.

'Westie, I couldn't stick it. I was only the office boy – told to run here, run there and

148

lick the stamps. It just wasn't my cup of tea.'

'Well, I can't think what Mr Holt will say.'

'That's why I didn't come round until I had got a new job all on my own,' Jim Holt said proudly. 'And, by the way, won't you introduce me?'

He waved his hand in Karina's direction.

'We are busy, Mr Jim,' Miss Weston said severely.

'Not too busy for a teeny weeny little introduction surely?'

'Very well then,' Miss Weston said crisply. 'Miss Burke, this is Mr Jim Holt.'

Jim Holt walked across the room and shook Karina by the hand.

'I'm the black sheep of the family,' he announced. 'I'm Garland's reprehensible and most incorrigible cousin. I think he's really rather ashamed of me. What do you think, Westie?'

'He's not ashamed of you,' Miss Weston replied, 'but he will be very disappointed at your throwing up that job.'

'You sound exactly like my housemaster at Eton,' Jim Holt said with an incorrigible smile. 'He was always disappointed in me. I used to wonder why he went on hoping against hope that I should ever be better.'

He turned to Karina.

'How have you managed to get into the holy of holies?'

'Mr Holt was kind enough to say Miss

Weston would look after me,' Karina replied.

'Ye gods! Garland hasn't fallen in love at last, has he?' Jim Holt enquired. 'I've never heard him give a helping hand to a woman before, and certainly not to anyone who looks like you.'

Karina felt the colour come into her face even while she couldn't help laughing. There was something infectious about Jim Holt's smile and his ridiculously frivolous way of talking.

'Of course there's nothing like that,' Karina replied. 'I ... I hardly know Mr Holt. I only happened to be staying at his house this last weekend and...'

'Heavens! You were there when the burglary took place!' Jim Holt interrupted. 'You're just the person I want to see. What happened? The papers are full of it. Did they really get away with all the contents of Aladdin's Cave?'

'Not all of them,' Karina told him.

'I bet Garland is as mad as fire,' Jim Holt went on. 'Very possessive is our Garland about his treasures. I remember him slapping me when I was a baby because I wanted to suck the paint off his tin soldiers.'

'Really, Mr Jim, I don't believe a word of it,' Miss Weston interposed. 'And I don't want to seem disagreeable but Miss Burke and I are very busy.'

'Miss Burke isn't going to be too busy to

150

tell me all about the burglary,' Jim Holt declared. 'Besides, I'm entitled to hear about it. I'm one of the family. I would have telephoned and asked myself if I hadn't thought they would refuse to accept a reversed charge.'

'Miss Burke can tell you about it another time but not now,' Miss Weston said. 'And I've got a lot of private calls to make so I must ask you to go.'

'If you have private calls to make, you know you do them in Garland's office,' Jim Holt said mischievously. 'You're just trying to keep Miss Burke from me.'

'If you haven't got any work to do,' Miss Weston replied ominously, '–we have.'

'All right, I'll go on one condition,' Jim Holt said. 'And that is that you both come and have lunch with me. What about it, Westie?'

'I'm sorry, but I am engaged,' Miss Weston answered. 'Thank you all the same.'

'What about you?' Jim Holt asked directly to Karina.

'I … I don't think I can,' she stammered.

'Why not?' he asked. 'Are you lunching with anyone else?'

He saw the answer in her face and added:

'No, of course you're not. You haven't fixed up anything your first day. You were thinking of sneaking out to some revolting sandwich bar and having a bun and a cup of

151

coffee. All that is very bad for you. My mother always said so. I'll fetch you at one o'clock and give you a decent meal. It won't be at the Ritz, but at least it will be better than the sandwich bar.'

Karina looked across the room at Miss Weston.

'I ... I don't know ... what to say,' she faltered.

This was something she had not expected. She felt that she ought not to accept an invitation from Jim Holt; and yet, at the same time, it seemed so difficult to say no when, as he guessed all too clearly, she had nowhere to go.

'That's settled then,' he said. 'One o'clock. I'll meet you in the hall downstairs. And don't let Westie put you off me. I may be bad, but no one could be as bad as I'm painted.'

He opened the door.

'Goodbye, Westie. If I don't see you again, put in a good word for me with the big man. I don't want him cutting me off with a shilling or anything like that.'

'It's what you deserve,' Miss Weston said sternly.

'Oh, Westie, have a heart!' Jim Holt cried and shut the door quietly behind him.

Miss Weston laughed.

'He's hopeless, isn't he?' she said to Karina.

'He seemed very happy about it all,' Karina replied.

'Oh, Jim Holt never takes anything seriously,' Miss Weston told her. 'He's had three jobs this year already, and as soon as they bore him he chucks them up. Mr Holt will be very upset about this last one. He had hoped that Mr Jim might settle down at last.'

'There doesn't seem much resemblance between them,' Karina said.

'Nevertheless they are first cousins,' Miss Weston replied. 'Mr Jim Holt's father and Mr Garland's father were brothers. I believe, though, that Mr Jim's father – like his son – was a spendthrift all his life. Anyway, if it wasn't for Mr Garland he would be completely penniless.'

'He's kind to his family, then?' Karina asked.

This was somehow a sidelight she had not expected to Garland Holt's character.

'Yes, he's very conscious of his responsibilities,' Miss Weston said primly and picked up the telephone again.

Karina felt embarrassed when, going down in the lift at lunch-time, Beth said to her:

'Will you come and have lunch with me? I usually go to a little place round the corner where it's not so crowded.'

'I should love to another day if I may,'

153

Karina answered. 'I'm going out to lunch today.'

'Oh, aren't you lucky!' Beth said. 'I always long for someone to ask me out.'

She would have said more if at that moment the lift had not stopped at the outer hall and Karina saw that Jim Holt was waiting there.

'Here you are,' he said. 'I was beginning to be frightened that you had avoided me by going down the fire escape.'

'I think really I ought to go out with one of the girls who has just asked me,' Karina said in a low voice, then looked round to find that Beth had already disappeared.

'You oughtn't to do anything you don't want to do,' Jim Holt said. 'You know, if you're honest, that you'd much rather have lunch with me. I've sold a car this morning and so it will be a good one. I drew my commission at the office in case the chap changes his mind and brings it back.'

He had a car outside – a small, open two-seater – and Karina was glad to see it had stopped raining.

'This is the only car they would let me pinch from the place where I'm working,' Jim explained. 'I took a Bentley out yesterday and got one of the wings bashed in. They were extremely annoyed about it. You'd have thought I'd done it on purpose.'

He chattered gaily until they arrived at a

small restaurant in a side street where he could park the car.

'If you like really good cooking, this is the place,' he told her.

He was obviously well known in the restaurant, for the proprietor greeted him with delight and led them to a comfortable table by the window. Jim Holt ordered cocktails despite Karina's protestations that she never drank at lunch-time, and then ordered a meal which, while it sounded delicious, made her feel that she would never get through it.

'I have got to work this afternoon,' she expostulated.

'Don't you let Westie drive you too hard,' Jim Holt said. 'She herself loves work, as other women love their husbands or their children. In fact, work is her only love. I used to think that she had a passion for Garland. But now I've decided she thinks of him as a kind of symbolic son, someone whom she can push to power.'

'I shouldn't have thought he wanted any pushing,' Karina said.

'That's all you know,' Jim answered. 'He's been pushed all his life – first and foremost by our grandmother! Have you met her, by the way?'

'Mrs de Winton? Yes, I met her.'

'She's a real old battle-axe,' Jim went on, 'consumed by ambitious fire and the determination to succeed when everyone else fails, and all that sort of thing. She's used Garland as an instrument for her own aspirations since she first realised how clever he is. She had it all planned out long before he left school. He was to carry on where her husband had left off. She never had much use for her sons. But Garland was everything she needed to forge ahead with her fantastic plans for an empire composed entirely of wealth.'

'You make it sound frightening,' Karina said.

'It is frightening,' Jim agreed. 'What is the point of money unless you are spending it? What fun does Garland get out of life?'

'Well, he has his home and all those lovely things around him,' Karina said.

'He hasn't bought a quarter of them; he hasn't even had the fun of going shopping for himself,' Jim said. 'They were all inherited or else grandmother purchased them. No, Garland has a rotten life if you ask me. I'm so sorry for him that sometimes I really feel like crying.'

Karina stared at him in amazement. This was somehow the last thing she expected to hear.

'You're sorry for him!' she said. 'But I thought you had no money.'

'I haven't, and I don't really want it,' Jim answered. 'As long as I have got enough to keep body and soul together, as long as I can earn a few pounds to take a pretty girl out to lunch, that's all I ask of life.'

He laughed at her amazed expression and went on:

'Oh, Garland's done his best for me. He's tried to put me into all sorts of businesses – and you know as well as I do that if Garland Holt says they've got to take a chap they take him. If I'd toed the line and been a good boy I should have been a rich man by now.'

'Don't you want to be rich?' Karina asked.

'What, and look like Garland?' he enquired. 'Not on your life. He's harassed, worried, weighed down with responsibilities and all the time being chivvied by women.'

'I don't think that's true,' Karina argued, 'except where his grandmother is concerned. He's frightened of women; he runs away from them. Everybody has told me that if a woman so much as looks at him he does his best never to see her again.'

'That's true,' Jim said. 'Perfectly true. But have you heard the reason why?'

'No, why?' Karina asked curiously.

She felt somehow that she ought not to be listening to all this, and yet Jim's confidences were irresistible.

'Well, after Garland had just begun to build up his fortune he fell in love. He must have been twenty-three at the time.'

'Was she pretty?' Karina asked quickly.

'Isn't that just like a woman? Yes, of course she was pretty – quite understandingly so,' Jim answered. 'And she had breeding and brains as well. Her father was an earl, but she wasn't just one of those stupid, goofy débutantes. She had been to Oxford, got a degree and had even begun to write a book. Everyone said it would be a perfect match.'

'And why wasn't it?' Karina asked. 'Did she die or something?'

'It would have been better for Garland if she had,' Jim replied. 'No, he discovered about three weeks before the wedding that she was only marrying him for his money. She had another boy-friend tucked away with whom she was really in love – penniless, charming and not even in the right sort of society.'

'How awful!' Karina exclaimed.

'It was for Garland,' Jim told her. 'Some kind friend took the trouble to tell him that his fiancée was spending the week-end at an obscure hotel in the New Forest. He motored down and found them there. There was no denying what they were up to and they admitted quite frankly they were in love with each other.'

'Oh, poor, poor Mr Holt!' Karina exclaimed.

'I've never seen a chap take it so hard,' Jim said. 'Then he went back to work and from

158

that day to this he's never discussed it with anyone.'

'And what happened to the girl?' Karina asked.

'Oh, she married someone else. Not the man she was in love with – another rich man, an American as it happens, and now she lives in the States.'

'But Mr Holt never got over it,' Karina said softly. 'This explains a lot of things.'

'I suppose some people would call it a blessing in disguise,' Jim went on. 'It made him work harder and made him concentrate on his business. They tell me he's one of the richest men in England today – I shouldn't be surprised.'

'It must have made him feel that he could never trust anyone again,' Karina said.

'I expect it did,' Jim replied. 'But he must have trusted you to let you into Miss Weston's office. It is really what one might call the inner sanctum. No one's ever got in there before.'

'I think he felt I was too insignificant to do any harm,' Karina smiled.

'Well, I tell you what I think,' Jim replied. 'That you are too pretty to be working. It's going to get you into a lot of trouble.'

'I don't see why,' Karina answered.

'Well, for one thing, every man you meet will want to make love to you.'

Karina laughed.

'Now you are being ridiculous.'

'No, it's true,' he said. 'And I am going to start right away. I think you are adorable – the most adorable person I have seen in years.'

There was so much sincerity in his voice that Karina's laugh was a little embarrassed.

'Now you are really are being ridiculous,' she said.

'You have got to believe me,' Jim answered. 'You could have knocked me down with a feather when I saw you in that office this morning. I felt you couldn't be real, that I must be seeing things. You are so pretty; much too pretty to wear out your eyes poring over Garland's tedious business letters. Where have you been hidden all these years?'

'I have been living in the country,' Karina said.

'Well, thank goodness you have come to London,' he answered. 'Karina, I mean this in all sincerity, you will let me see something of you, won't you?'

'I ... I don't know,' Karina began, feeling it was exciting to have someone flirting with her in this ardent manner, but still not sure of what she should do or what she should say. It was the first time in her life it had ever happened to her.

And then, as she hesitated for words, she saw Jim glance up quickly and a little smile curve the corners of his mouth.

'The great man himself,' he murmured.

Karina turned her head. Garland Holt had just come into the restaurant. He had two other men with him, both obviously businessmen. She saw him glance round the room casually, and then a look of surprise came into his face.

Leaving his friends, he walked across to where she and Jim were sitting.

'What are you doing here?' he asked.

'Good morning, Garland!' Jim replied. 'Isn't it rather obvious? I am taking Miss Burke out to lunch.'

'So I see,' Garland Holt replied sharply. And Karina knew that for some inexplicable reason he was extremely annoyed.

CHAPTER SEVEN

Karina stared at herself in the looking-glass. She had never seen herself look so different, so unlike the ordinary Karina who usually stared back at her and whom she knew so well.

This was someone quite new, someone who still was small and fairylike, but who yet managed to look sophisticated in a gown of blue and silver lace which shimmered round her like moonlight on the sea.

So much seemed to have happened today that she could hardly remember in what sequence the events had crowded one on top of the other – and what was more, she could hardly believe they were true.

She had found it difficult to enjoy her lunch with Jim Holt even though it had been an excitement in itself to go out to lunch in a London restaurant alone with a young man. From the moment that Garland Holt had arrived she had felt that his dark eyes were boring into her back.

She found it hard even to taste the delicious food. She kept glancing at her little gold wrist-watch in case she should be a minute late back at the office.

'I hope my cousin is not leading you into bad ways your first day in the City,' Garland Holt had said in a disagreeable voice.

'I won't be late back,' Karina murmured, feeling as if she had already committed a fault and knowing that he was angry by the way his dark eyebrows seemed almost to meet across the bridge of his nose.

He then turned his attention to Jim.

'I hear you have left the stockbrokers,' he said.

Jim smiled disarmingly.

'That's exactly what I came to tell you this morning, but if you know it already there is no need for me to make a humble confession.'

'I met one of the partners half an hour ago,' Garland Holt explained. 'He was extremely disappointed that you have left, and so am I. I went to a lot of trouble to get you in, Jim.'

'I know, Garland, and I'm grateful, I am really. But it just wasn't my cup of tea. I've got myself a job.'

'What is it?'

The question came like a pistol shot.

'Selling cars for Wedbury and Kent.'

'Do you call touting on commission a job?' Garland Holt asked sarcastically.

'It gives me a chance of meeting people. It's no use, Garland; the only virtue I've got is the human touch. It's something you often lack yourself, old boy.'

Garland Holt turned away from the table.

'I will talk to you about that another time,' he said. 'Kindly don't be late back at the office, Karina.'

With that he left them. But Karina was acutely conscious of him. He was right at the other end of the room, but all the time she felt he was actually with them at the table.

'Stop worrying,' Jim told her. 'What the hell does it matter what he thinks or says? You're pretty enough to get a job anywhere, and a far better one than licking stamps for old Westie.'

'You don't understand,' Karina said. 'I'm not really qualified for anything.'

'With a face like that you don't need to be,' he answered.

He paid her extravagant compliments, and though she laughed at them and told him he was ridiculous, she could not help feeling flattered. Never before had she been able to be on such easy terms with a young man. If men of her own age had come to Letchfield Park, there had always been Aunt Margaret or Cyril at her side, keeping them away from her, making, in some extraordinary manner of their own, a barrier between herself and the outside world.

Now, as she laughed and even blushed at Jim's compliments, she felt young and carefree. It was all such fun, so unlike anything she had ever known before. At the same time, the hands of the clock never let her forget for a moment that she must be back at the office on time.

She made Jim hurry over his coffee and the brandy that he insisted on having with it. She fidgeted while he paid the bill and then sprang to her feet.

'Don't bother to come with me,' she said. 'I'll find my own way.'

'Nonsense,' he answered. 'As if I would let you go out in the street alone looking like that! Besides, the car is waiting. Think how disappointed it would be if it didn't see you again.'

'You are absurd!' Karina answered, but she was laughing as she moved from the table.

And then, as she turned, she found herself looking into Garland Holt's angry eyes. The smile faded from her lips. She hurried towards the door, with Jim following her in a more leisurely fashion.

'Hurry! Hurry!' she said when they reached the car. 'I feel that in some clever way of his own he will get there before I do and be waiting for me in the office.'

'Don't be frightened of him,' Jim advised, and then he bent over to squeeze her hand. 'I know exactly how you feel. I have been terrified of him for years. He always makes me feel as if I am at school again and have been sent for by the prefect to get six of the best.'

'It is ridiculous, really,' Karina said. 'He's not so very much older than we are.'

'He's only eighteen months older than I am,' Jim answered. 'But you are a baby.'

'I'm not,' she said indignantly. 'I shall be twenty-one in four weeks' time.'

'Good lord!' Jim said. 'I had no idea. I thought you had just left school.'

'I suppose I ought to take that as a compliment,' Karina replied. 'But I am sick of being told how young I look. I want to be old and sophisticated. I want people to think I am wise instead of stupid.'

Jim threw back his head and laughed.

'Women are never satisfied,' he said. 'I'll tell you one thing. If you are as old as you say you are, then you can do as you like. Don't be pushed about by anyone. Just enjoy yourself and be young while you can. We shall all be old one day.'

'Is that your whole philosophy?' Karina enquired.

'All of it,' he agreed. 'Let's laugh and be merry, for tomorrow we die – or, worse than dying, we get old and nobody wants us.'

'In the meantime we have got to eat,' Karina said. 'And though you don't seem to mind changing your job whenever it suits you, this is my first job and I mean to make a success of it. So hurry, please, hurry!'

'On one condition.'

'What's that?'

'That you dine with me tonight.'

'Oh, I don't think I could.'

'Why not? What else are you going to do? Sit in your lodgings and twiddle your thumbs?'

She had already told him that she was staying with Mr and Mrs Carter, and now that he put it like that it did seem rather a gloomy outlook for her second night in London.

She was tempted to accept Jim's invitation even though she could not help remembering how shocked Aunt Margaret would be at her going out twice in the same day with a man she hardly knew.

'That's a date then,' Jim said. 'Otherwise I am going to drive at ten miles an hour so that you will be late at the office.'

'You're blackmailing me,' Karina exclaimed.

'All's fair in love and war, Karina; you know that, don't you?'

'Even though I am a country bumpkin I don't want you to make fun of me,' she answered.

'I'm not making fun of you,' he replied and his voice was serious. 'The moment I walked into that office something very peculiar happened inside me.'

168

'Indigestion!' Karina said, striving to speak in the same light manner that he had been using a few moments before.

He shook his head.

'No,' he said. 'It was love at first sight. I know now what the women novelists mean when they say, "his heart leapt and turned over", or whatever term they use. It really happened to me.'

'Please, Jim, I am going to be late,' Karina pleaded, because there didn't seem anything else that she could say.

'All right,' he said in his more normal, frivolous tone. 'I'll tell you about it tonight. But just think of me between now and then, will you? It will seem the hell of a long time to me.'

He drew up outside the big building where Garland Holt had his offices. Karina held out her hand. He gave it a quick squeeze and then, looking into her eyes, said:

'You're lovely! I'm mad about you. I'll pick you up at eight o'clock, and don't be a minute late for me because I just couldn't bear it.'

'I'll be ready,' Karina said with a smile. 'And thank you for asking me.'

She pulled her hand from his and ran up the steps and into the big hall with its lifts and glass doors. It seemed to her that the lift was unaccountably slow in reaching the eighth floor. She hurried into the office to find, to her relief, that only some of the girls were back and Miss Weston was not in her room.

Karina took off her coat and hung it up, tidied her hair and then went to her desk. She was typing demurely when the door opened and Garland Holt came in.

'So you are back, are you?' he said in what she felt was a rather disagreeable tone.

'Yes, Mr Holt,' she answered.

He opened the door of his own room.

'Come in here, Karina. I wish to speak to you for a moment.'

As she rose to her feet she remembered how Jim had said that Garland always made him feel as if he were a schoolboy again. It was like going into the headmaster's study, Karina thought now.

She went into the smaller room, closing the door behind her. Garland was sitting at his desk, a pile of papers in front of him. He got up when she entered and walked restlessly to the window, and she had an impression that he was trying to find words.

She waited. He did not ask her to sit down, and she thought in her capacity as an assistant in the office she must remain standing.

'How did you meet my cousin Jim?' Garland Holt asked at length, turning from the window to face her.

'I met him here, this morning, in this

170

office,' Karina answered.

'And you went out to lunch with him?'

'Well ... he ... asked me,' Karina said.

'Asked you?' Garland Holt queried. 'Do you always do anything anyone asks you? Do you usually accept invitations from a man you don't know?'

'Well ... he was your cousin and ... and Miss Weston introduced us,' Karina said.

'It is absolutely ridiculous,' Garland Holt snapped. 'Jim is not at all the type of man you should be seen about with.'

Karina couldn't help smiling.

'Nobody knows me in London,' she said. 'I don't think there will be anyone to see me or make any comments about who I'm with.'

'I feel a responsibility for you, don't you understand?' Garland Holt asked, hitting the top of a chair with his fist. 'Jim is hopeless, irresponsible and extravagant. The only thing he has managed to get for himself is a bad reputation where women are concerned. You are not to go out with him, do you understand?'

'Oh ... but he has ... been very kind to me,' Karina said. 'I don't think I could throw him over just because...'

'Throw him over!' Garland Holt interrupted. 'What do you mean? He has asked you to go out again?'

'Yes, tonight,' Karina replied, feeling

somehow embarrassed even as she said it.

'You must be crazy or very badly brought up,' Garland Holt said. 'I always thought that a girl got to know someone before she went gallivanting out with him.'

'Well, I really didn't see why I shouldn't,' Karina said. 'It's better than sitting in my lodgings.'

'So you are in lodgings, are you?' Garland Holt enquired.

'Yes, at 25 Blackdale Street, with Cousin Felix's valet and his wife. It's near Paddington. They are very kind and it is quite comfortable, but it is not very exciting.'

'Exciting! Do you want things to be exciting?' Garland Holt enquired. 'I should have thought you would have had enough excitement in the last few days – running away from home; getting hit on the head by burglars; starting a new job. You can't want to add to all that by going out with Jim.'

Quite suddenly Karina felt rebellious. Why, she asked herself, should she be bullied by him? She didn't know Garland Holt much better than she knew Jim and there was no reason why she should submit to him making rules and regulations about her life just because he was employing her from nine till five.

'I am sorry if you are annoyed,' she said, 'but I think that I ought to be in the same position as all the other typists in your office. When they leave here, their private life is their own.'

'You mean I am not to interfere?' Garland Holt asked.

'I am sure you mean it very kindly,' Karina said softly. 'But I am old enough to look after myself.'

'Very well,' Garland said.

'Oh, please don't be angry,' she said quickly, feeling that she had been rude. 'You have been so very kind in giving me this chance, but I don't want to be a burden to you and you must see that I have got to grow up and look after myself now I am on my own.'

'You are so ridiculously young,' he said.

'I'm not,' Karina replied. 'I only look young. It's quite a different thing.'

'What experience have you had of men like Jim?' he asked.

There was no answer to this and she could only make a rather hopeless little shrug of her shoulders.

'Very well,' he said. 'You must do what you want to do. But you are not going to dine with Jim tonight for the simple reason that there is some work I want you to do.'

'Of course,' Karina replied. 'If you want me, Mr Holt, that is a very different thing. At what time do you expect to finish?'

'I have no idea,' Garland answered. 'But well after midnight, I should imagine.'

'After midnight!'

Karina could not help the surprise in her voice.

'Oh, we are not going to work here,' Garland explained. 'It is something which involves contacts with people outside. We have got to dine with them. I'll send a car to Blackdale Street for you at a quarter-past eight. I'm not quite certain where we shall be dining – the Savoy, I expect.'

'In ... evening dress?' Karina asked.

'Yes,' Garland replied.

He walked to his desk and picked up one of the papers which were in front of him.

'That will be all,' he said.

Karina, knowing she was dismissed, went back into the outer office. Miss Weston was back from lunch.

'Mr Holt is early,' she said. 'Did he want you to do something for him?'

'Only to put off the engagement I had made for this evening,' Karina answered. 'Do you know Mr Jim Holt's telephone number?'

'No, not his new one,' Miss Weston replied. 'Did Mr Holt know who you were dining with?'

'Yes, I told him.'

'Oh dear!' Miss Weston exclaimed. 'He didn't like it, I suppose? He doesn't approve of Mr Jim's goings-on and makes no secret of it.'

'He certainly doesn't,' Karina agreed. 'May I look up the number of Wedbury and Kent in the Directory and ring Mr Jim now?'

'You can,' Miss Weston said. 'But as a general rule it is best to make your private calls outside in the lunch hour.'

'Yes, of course, I understand,' Karina said.

She dialled the number but was told that Jim was not there. She left a message for him to ring her back and had just started to type again the letters that Miss Weston had given her when the telephone on her desk rang. She picked it up.

'May I speak to Miss Burke?' a voice asked, but before she answered she realised it was not Jim, whom she expected, but Felix who was calling her.

'Is that you, Cousin Felix?' she asked.

'Yes,' he replied. 'How are you getting on?'

'All right, I hope,' Karina said, feeling that Felix would not at all have approved of what had happened to her.

'Good,' Felix said. 'You won't find it too difficult when you get into it. Come along to dinner tonight and you can tell me all about it.'

'I can't,' Karina said.

'Why not?'

'Mr Holt wants me to go out with him.'

'The devil he does!'

'I'm sorry, Cousin Felix, but he says it's business.'

175

'Keeping you late at the office?'

'No, that's the whole trouble. He says he may be dining with some other people at the Savoy. Cousin Felix, I don't think I've got the right things to wear.'

'The Savoy, eh? Well, I'll see what I can do. Don't worry, Karina. I have a friend who's got a shop. I'll tell her to send something along to Carter's house. If it's too big, Mrs Carter can sew you into it.'

'Oh, but, Cousin Felix...' Karina began to expostulate, but he had already rung off.

How extraordinary he was, she thought. One moment making a fuss of her, the next minute seeming extremely glad that she was going out with Garland Holt. He was quite unfathomable. At the same time, she had to admit that he had exquisite taste and that if he did produce a dress for her it was certain to be something suitable and pretty.

She found the dress when she got back to the Carters' house. It was in a dress-box with quite a well-known name on it, and when she opened the box she gasped with excitement.

Never had she seen such a lovely dress; and with it there was a velvet wrap lined with swansdown to wear round her shoulders and a small velvet bag to match.

'Carter says Mr Mainwaring has been telephoning all the afternoon to get that for you,' Mrs Carter remarked.

'It is so kind of him,' Karina said. 'I have never seen such a wonderful dress before.'

'I expect it cost a bit,' Mrs Carter said admiringly. 'You can't buy a dress like that on the cheap.'

'I must thank him,' Karina said. 'Do you think he's at home now?'

'No,' Mrs Carter replied. 'My husband says he has gone out and won't be back for dinner.'

'I will write him a note,' Karina said, 'and perhaps your husband can take it round first thing in the morning so that Mr Mainwaring can have it on his breakfast tray.'

She tried the dress on and Mrs Carter found that with just taking it in an inch round the waist it fitted beautifully.

'It's always better to have things a little bit too big than too small,' Mrs Carter said. 'Now, if we'd had to let it out, that would have been difficult.'

'Mr Mainwaring was so clever to guess my measurements so exactly!' Karina exclaimed.

'He's very fussy about his own clothes,' Mrs Carter said. 'But then he's fussy about everything which isn't quite perfect. Many's the time I have felt myself getting real exasperated with him when he's complained because there's an ornament out of place or the merest speck of dust you can hardly see on the window-sill. But then, as Carter

always says, if you're employed by somebody like Mr Mainwaring it makes you take
a real pride in your work.'

'I wonder he's never married,' Karina said.

'Never seemed to care for women,' Mrs
Carter remarked. 'Oh, there are plenty of
them that he has for friends, but I've never
known him in love. A good thing, if you ask
me. Carter wouldn't stay if there was a
mistress in the flat. He don't hold with
working for women.'

'I'm sure Mr Mainwaring would be
miserable if Carter left him,' Karina said.
'He speaks so very highly of him.'

'Carter's got himself dug into that job,'
Mrs Carter said, 'and it's not surprising. Mr
Mainwaring's a real gentleman, I'll say that
for him.'

Karina could not help smiling at the
phrase. She had heard it so often before.

'Your uncle is a real gentleman!' the gar-
deners and grooms at Letchfield Park used
to say. And it usually meant that Uncle
Simon had congratulated them on something they had done or given them an extra
bonus for Christmas.

They had never said anything like that
about Aunt Margaret because she was
usually the one who found fault.

'Mrs Carter, would you mind if I used the
telephone?' Karina asked.

'No, dear. You'll find a box to put the

178

threepence in if it's a local call and a pad to write it down on if it's a trunk. You pays for them when the bill comes in.'

Karina went to the telephone. For the sixth time that day she tried to get hold of Jim; but now there was no reply from the showrooms and instead she rang his club, the name of which Miss Weston had given her before she left the office.

'Mr Jim Holt is not in,' the porter told her.

Karina left her number and an urgent message for him to telephone her. It was so awful, after all his kindness, that not only was she letting him down but that she was unable to tell him she could not come.

Time crept on, but the telephone did not ring. Much too early she started to change her clothes, principally because she longed to see herself in the blue and silver dress.

And now, looking into the mirror, she was amazed at the transformation it made. Always before she had worn plain, simple, little-girl dresses. It was not exactly a question of choice; it was because she was too small to wear anything else. If she went shopping with Aunt Margaret they were forced to go to the Junior Miss Department, and the only alternative was to have things made by the village dressmaker who was incapable of doing anything more elaborate than a dress with a plain bodice and a full skirt.

This dress made her look grown-up; and to be in keeping with its cleverly draped bodice and tiny waist, Karina brushed her hair high on her head, adding several inches to her height.

'It's a lovely dress, there's no mistake about that,' Mrs Carter said, as she helped Karina into it. 'You look real pretty, miss. I'm sorry Carter has gone out. I should have liked him to see you.'

'It's a wonderful dress, isn't it, Mrs Carter?' Karina cried. 'I can't thank Mr Mainwaring enough for giving me anything so wonderful!'

'I expect he had his reasons, miss,' Mrs Carter remarked in a slightly dry tone.

Karina stood still for a moment. It was true, she thought. Cousin Felix wouldn't have done anything without a reason. What could his reason be? Why should he be so anxious for her to look nice tonight when she was going out with Garland Holt and not with him?

She wished she understood her cousin better. She wished, at the same time, that she liked him more. There was something about him, something from which she shrank instinctively.

'Stop! Stop!' she told herself. 'You are being disloyal. You are being horrid about a man who's shown you only the greatest kindness and consideration.'

With her dress billowing out around her she sat down at the table and wrote Felix a little note.

'*Thank you a thousand times,*' she ended. '*You have been so wonderful to me about everything. I can never be sufficiently grateful.*

'*Yours,*
'*Karina.*'

As she put it in an envelope ready for Carter to take round to the flat the next morning, she heard the front-door bell ring. She looked at the clock over the mantelpiece. It was only five minutes to eight.

'That will be Mr Jim,' she said to Mrs Carter. 'Mr Garland Holt said he wouldn't be here until a quarter past.'

'You can have a word with him in the front room, miss,' Mrs Carter said. 'There's not a fire there, but it won't be cold if you put your wrap round you.'

Karina picked up her wrap and ran down the stairs. Mrs Carter opened the door. Jim came in. He was not in evening clothes and his eyes widened when he saw Karina.

'What a fool I am!' he exclaimed. 'I didn't say we were going dancing and I thought you wouldn't have changed.'

'I am so sorry,' Karina said, 'but everything has gone wrong. I can't come out with you tonight.'

'Not come out with me?' Jim enquired. 'Then why are you dressed like that? Who's taking you out?'

'Mr Holt,' Karina answered.

Jim shut the door behind him and, chucking his hat and stick down on a chair, said:

'Blast Garland! I know what he's up to. I suppose he thinks he's being clever. Did he give you that dress?'

'No, of course not,' Karina answered. 'Do you think I would take a present of that sort from him? Cousin Felix gave it to me.'

'When?' Jim enquired.

'This afternoon. He also asked me out to dinner. I have been quite popular today. When I told him that I was going out on a business evening with Mr Holt and had nothing to wear he sent me round this dress.'

'So that's Felix's little game, is it?'

'I don't know what you mean.'

'Never mind,' Jim answered. 'It's Garland who concerns me. Did he ask you to dinner because he knew I was taking you out?'

Karina nodded.

'He hates me,' Jim said briefly. 'Always has done, if it comes to that. I really believe it's jealousy. He does nothing but work and I get all the fun. Besides, once I took a girl-friend away from him. He's just like an elephant. He neither forgives nor forgets.'

'I'm very sorry,' Karina said again, 'but there was nothing I could do, was there? He said he wanted me because it was business.'

'Oh, it will be business all right,' Jim said. 'Garland never thinks of anything else. But it would also be good business for him if, where a woman was concerned, he could spite me and put a spoke in my wheel. He's all right in every other way – gets me jobs, lends me money – but he disapproves of my success with girls. Didn't you see him glaring at us at lunch today?'

'It all seems rather silly to me,' Karina said with what she hoped was dignity. 'After all, we had only met today for the first time.'

'It wouldn't have mattered if it had been the fifty-fifth time,' Jim said. 'Garland would have tried to save you from my evil influence. He really believes I'm a modern Don Juan-cum-Casanova. Pathetic, isn't it?'

'And aren't you?' Karina asked with a little smile.

Jim smiled back.

'I hope I am where you are concerned,' he replied. 'Dine with me tomorrow night? But don't tell Garland, otherwise he will trump up another excuse to keep you at his side.'

'It does seem rather silly,' Karina said. 'Perhaps he really wants me.'

'Don't kid yourself,' Jim answered. 'Where I'm concerned Garland behaves like a cross between a policeman and a Calvinistic

183

minister. He can't help it – and he has his virtues as well as his faults.'

'I tried to get you all the afternoon on the telephone to warn you,' Karina said.

'I have been busy,' Jim replied briefly. 'As a matter of fact, I have sold another car to an old chum of mine and we were sitting in the Ritz cracking a bottle over the deal. And that, I may tell you, is the sort of way that Garland thinks business should not be done.'

'I am glad you sold another car,' Karina said.

Jim smiled at her.

'And I'm glad that you are the loveliest thing that has come into my life for years. You look so adorable in that dress that I have a very good mind to elope with you right away and then let Garland see what he can do about it.'

'I've made a resolution not to run away from anything any more!' Karina laughed.

'I'm asking you to run with me,' Jim answered.

'No running,' Karina said firmly.

'Very well, we'll do it all in the sedate and traditional manner. I'll call for you tomorrow night and you must come out with me in that dress and I'll tell you from eight o'clock until at least two in the morning that I adore you.'

'And I shall try not to believe a word of it,'

Karina said.

'I'll make you,' he replied. 'Shall I show you how?'

He stepped towards her, but Karina was too quick for him. She put a chair between them and, laughing at him over the top, said:

'This isn't at all the sedate or traditional manner.'

'Karina, you drive me mad!' Jim said, suddenly dropping his bantering tone. 'I have been thinking about you the whole afternoon.'

'Even while you were selling the car?' she teased him.

'Of course, why else do you think I want the money?' he said. 'I want to spend it on you.'

A clock somewhere in the house made a little chiming sound. Karina gave a sudden exclamation.

'You must go away at once,' she said. 'I can't think what I'm doing letting you stay here. Mr Holt is coming at a quarter-past eight. He'll be furious if he finds you here.'

'I don't care what Garland thinks one way or another,' Jim retorted.

'Yes you do,' Karina said quickly. 'He's your cousin and he's kind to you. You have got no money and he's very rich. You mustn't quarrel with him, of course you mustn't. Also he's my employer. Go away, please go away at once.'

Jim seemed suddenly to see sense.

'All right. I'll be good, but only until tomorrow night.'

He picked up his hat and then suddenly turned towards Karina and before she realised what he was doing he had reached her side and pulled her into his arms.

'You're utterly and completely fascinating,' he said. 'I shall be able to think of nothing else all night.'

Before she could move, before she could evade him, he had kissed her. His lips were warm and passionate on hers. His arms tightened around her shoulders and she felt as if he squeezed the breath out of her body.

For a moment she was unable to move. She was hypnotised by him, held by some inertia which she could not explain even to herself. And then as suddenly as he had taken her in his arms she was free.

'I love you!' he said, his voice deep and moved; and before she could say anything or even realise what had happened he had gone from the room, shutting the door behind him.

She heard him open the front door, heard it slam. Very slowly she put her hand up to her lips. She had been kissed – her first kiss – by a man she had only met at lunch-time. And yet she told herself that she felt as if she had known Jim all her life. There was something so gay, so irresponsible about him.

She had known that her lips, even if they had not responded to his, had not repulsed him. So that was what kissing was like, she thought to herself – that sudden moment of breathlessness, that inexplicable closeness in which her mouth had been utterly captive to his.

She could hear again his voice saying, in a tone that was low and deep and very unlike his usual laughing voice: 'I love you!'

Was this really love at first sight? Did she love him? What did she feel about him? She didn't know. She only knew that she felt a little uncertain and bewildered by everything that had happened. She could still feel Jim's lips on hers, could still feel the strength of his arms around her shoulders.

There was a peal of the electric bell. Garland Holt must have arrived; and now, in a sudden panic, she felt that she could not meet him. She must have time to think, a moment to breathe.

It was too late! Mrs Carter had answered the door. Karina heard her voice and then Garland Holt's. The door of the sitting-room opened.

'Mr Holt, miss!' Mrs Carter announced.

Karina felt as if she were caught. She wanted to run away; she wanted to avoid seeing him. Why, she did not know. But already he was in the room.

'Good evening, Karina!'

His voice was grave and yet there was a sudden light in his eyes. She wondered why. With a great effort she forced her thoughts away from Jim and towards him. She saw him staring at her; and then, with what was almost a shock of surprise, she realised that it was admiration she saw in his face and that, quite spontaneously, he was admiring her in her new dress.

CHAPTER EIGHT

Garland Holt helped Karina into the big chauffeur-driven car and sat down beside her.

'You look very smart,' he said in a voice that somehow struck her as being suspicious.

'Cousin Felix gave me this dress,' she replied.

Garland said nothing for a moment and then he asked:

'What does your cousin mean to you? Are you very fond of him?'

Karina was surprised at the question. She turned her face towards him and in the light of the street lamps she could see that he was staring down at her, frowning.

'Cousin Felix has been very kind to me,' she said. 'If it hadn't been for him I should … have been married at this moment.'

She shivered as she spoke.

'To the man I saw you with three years ago on the balcony in Belgrave Square?' Garland asked.

'How can you remember that?' Karina asked. 'And why did you remember me?'

He did not answer her for a moment, as if

he was debating whether to tell her the truth, and then he said:

'You sounded helpless and unhappy. There was something in your voice – I can't explain exactly what – which remained in my mind. I used to wonder afterwards what you would have said if I had asked you to dance.'

'I should have been very glad if you had,' Karina replied. 'I hated all the dances I went to that summer because I never seemed to have any partners – except Cyril.'

'Don't think about it now,' Garland said sharply. 'It is past and it is never any use regretting. You must learn to cut your losses. I have always believed that was the first and most important lesson any financier should absorb.'

'But I am not a financier,' Karina said with a little smile.

'No, but the same applies to life,' Garland said. 'Far too many people keep looking back. "If only I'd done so and so…" "If only I hadn't made a fool of myself over this or that." What is past is past. It's the future that counts.'

He spoke so violently that the whole car seemed to vibrate with the power of his voice.

'Don't you ever regret anything you've done?' Karina asked.

'Yes, of course,' he said almost roughly. 'If

I didn't, I should not feel so strongly about it. I've made many mistakes in my life – who hasn't? I know that one shouldn't think about them, but, of course, I do.'

'I'm glad,' she said involuntarily.

'Glad?' he asked quickly. 'What do you mean by glad?'

She flushed at the question.

'I think I meant that I was glad that you are so human. Just like me and all the other people who know that they shouldn't do something and yet go on doing it.'

Garland put back his head and laughed.

'You always say something I don't expect; it's a novelty. I assure you.'

'I'm afraid it is only because I'm not sophisticated and worldly wise,' Karina said.

'But you are not as young as you look.'

'No, that's true,' she admitted.

'It might be a useful asset at times.'

'That's what Cousin Felix said.'

She felt Garland stiffen and wondered what she had said that was wrong. 'He must dislike Cousin Felix very much.' She thought and made a mental reservation not to mention him if she could possibly help it. It was obvious that the mere mention of his name had taken away Garland's desire to confide in her.

They said little more until the car drew up at the Savoy. Garland helped her out and they went through the big swing-doors into the vestibule. A liveried attendant showed Karina the way to the ladies' cloakroom, where she left her wrap and glanced at herself for a moment in the big, shining mirrors.

She felt that her new dress gave her confidence. She was not so afraid of Garland as she had been. She was not so apprehensive about what lay ahead.

'It's exciting,' she told her reflection. 'Exciting to be in the Savoy and to be meeting new people. If I were at home...' And then she remembered who would have been with her if she had been at home.

She turned abruptly from the mirror and went outside into the crowd and chatter of the people sitting round drinking cocktails before they went into the restaurant. She saw Garland talking to a man and woman and moved across to his side.

'Oh, here you are, Karina,' he said. 'Mrs Westenholtz, may I introduce Miss Karina Burke?'

A very pretty, exquisitely dressed American girl held out her hand.

'I'm pleased to meet you, Miss Burke,' she said. 'I'll have you know my husband, Carl Westenholtz. We're from Pittsburgh.'

Garland ushered them to a table, where he ordered cocktails. Then they were led into the main dining-room and given a flower-decorated table beside the dance floor.

Mrs Westenholtz never drew breath. She talked about herself and her husband and how they had only been married for three months. She talked about New York and their trip to Europe, about their house in Pittsburgh and her husband's business.

Karina could not help being amused. She gathered amidst all the chatter that Carl Westenholtz and Garland Holt were doing business together, but it was quite obvious that they were not going to get a chance to speak while the vivacious bride talked for them.

Karina let her mind wander. She looked at the people dancing, she enjoyed the delicious food and sipped the pale golden champagne. It was all like a dream, she thought. 'I am Cinderella,' she told herself, 'and the only thing that is missing is Prince Charming.'

She could not help wishing that Jim was with her. It would be fun to listen to his extravagant compliments, to hear him flirting with her. She checked herself suddenly. Was it flirting or was it something more serious? Could she believe him?

'What are you thinking about?'

The question broke in upon her thoughts and she started guiltily.

'Oh, I ... I'm sorry,' she stammered.

'Mrs Westenholtz has asked you a question, Karina,' Garland said.

'I do apologise,' Karina said hastily, 'but I wasn't listening. I'm afraid I was watching the dancers. I have never been to the Savoy before and it's very fascinating for me.'

'Well, I can quite understand that,' Mrs Westenholtz said. 'I remember when I was first taken to the Waldorf Astoria...'

She was off again and Karina stole an anxious glance at Garland to see if he was really angry with her. To her relief, and a little to her surprise, his eyes were twinkling.

Finally, when dinner was over, Mrs Westenholtz suggested the ladies should go to the cloakroom. She led the way, and when they reached it she turned to Karina and said:

'You must forgive my being personal and saying how much I admire your dress. It's the prettiest thing I've ever seen.'

'Oh, thank you,' Karina said. 'It was given me as a present to wear tonight.'

'Well, it's really lovely,' Mrs Westenholtz said. 'And you're a lovely girl, too. I must be frank and say I was surprised when I saw you. Both Carl and I were expecting someone else.'

'Someone else?' Karina questioned.

Mrs Westenholtz nodded.

'Yes. Well, we sort of thought from the last time we were here that Mr Holt was keen on Lady Carol Byng, so we said to him: "Carl and I, being on our honeymoon, aren't

194

gonna be much company for you, so you bring along someone you fancy." And we were quite certain he'd bring Lady Carol.'

Karina was not quite certain why, but she felt a little deflated.

'I ... I'm sorry,' she murmured deprecatingly.

'Now you mustn't take it that way,' Mrs Westenholtz said. 'We're real glad to meet you, and I know Carl thinks you're as pretty as I do; and I'm quite certain Mr Holt wouldn't have asked you if he hadn't thought you were more important to him than Lady Carol.'

'No, I don't think it's like that at all,' Karina said. 'You see, I work in Mr Holt's office.'

'Well, isn't that just fine?' Mrs Westenholtz said. 'I've always said that men know the way to get themselves the prettiest secretaries. No wonder their wives are jealous. I shall tell Carl about this – and I won't let him engage anyone in future unless I see her.'

Karina laughed dutifully. At the same time she felt a little uncomfortable. This wasn't in the least the sort of dinner-party she had expected. She had thought that it would consist of the same heavy, elderly financiers who had been staying at Garland Holt's house all the weekend. She had become then quite skilful at listening to the older men droning on about their business experiences, and it had been a surprise to find that the dinner-party was merely one of four.

'I think Mr Holt is just too attractive for words,' Mrs Westenholtz was saying. 'There's something about that reserved British type which just makes my heart go pitter-pat. I've always told Carl that if he hadn't been so insistent about leading me up the aisle I'd have married a Britisher.'

'I don't think Mr Holt will ever marry anyone,' Karina said firmly. 'You see, he's so rich he thinks everyone is running after him for his money.'

'My, isn't that silly!' Mrs Westenholtz said. 'Why, Carl is as rich as he is, and I could name dozens more. Of course, in the States we girls like to catch a millionaire if we can get one, but they don't get a complex about it – we soon see to that.'

'There's one thing of which you can be quite certain,' Karina smiled. 'It is that Mr Holt will have someone different to bring out to dinner with you next time you ask him.'

'I certainly hope he doesn't,' Mrs Westenholtz replied. 'I've taken a real fancy to you, and you mustn't call me Mrs Westenholtz, you must call me Sadie. And I think your name is just cute.'

It was difficult, Karina thought, to be even the least bit reserved in the face of such overwhelming friendliness. And then, as she smiled at Sadie, the American thrust an arm through hers and said:

'Don't you be down-hearted, honey. You'll get him if you set your mind to it – and I don't blame you for being in love with him. He's just like a movie star.'

Karina stiffened.

'Oh, but please,' she said, 'you mustn't think I'm in love with Mr Holt – I'm not. I hardly know him. He asked me to come tonight because...' She stopped suddenly, wondering why Garland Holt had asked her.

Was it only because he didn't want her to go out with Jim or was it because he wanted her to meet his American friends? She was quite certain that the last reason was not the true one. Anyway, whatever the reason it wasn't a very complimentary one.

Sadie was quite unabashed.

'If you're not in love with him,' she said, 'you soon will be. And I shouldn't take too long about it either. As you've said yourself, there are lots of girls ready to run after a millionaire, especially when he's good-looking.'

Karina gave up the hopeless task of trying to explain to this voluble American what was the truth. It was even more difficult, she thought, because she didn't know herself what the truth was. She was sure of only one thing – that she didn't want to marry Garland Holt, not under any circumstances.

They went back to the table, Sadie still talking volubly, to find the men chatting over their cigars and large balloon glasses of brandy. They rose to their feet, a little reluctantly Karina thought, as if they were annoyed at being interrupted. But Sadie soon had the whole table listening to her again.

Finally Carl Westenholtz got to his feet.

'I want to dance,' he said. 'And if you'll forgive me, Miss Burke, I'm going to ask my wife first because I still count this trip as part of our honeymoon.'

'Now, isn't that the sweetest thing!' Sadie said. 'You see, Karina, what a honey of a husband I've got! You'll have to hurry up and get yourself one.'

She winked at Karina as she rose to her feet, then melted into her husband's arms on the dance floor, and they were soon lost from view amongst the crowd doing the samba.

'What does she mean by that?' Garland asked curiously.

'I have no idea,' Karina said untruthfully, blushing as she spoke.

'Does she think there is something between us?' Garland asked in an amused voice.

'Once she made up her mind,' Karina

198

replied, 'nothing I could say would alter it.'

'No, I gather that,' Garland said.

'As a matter of fact,' Karina went on, feeling that the conversation was embarrassing, but that it would be worse to leave so many things unsaid between them, 'Mrs Westenholtz was expecting Lady Carol to come with you tonight.'

'Yes, I know she was,' Garland said. 'I am afraid poor Carl is married to a romantic. They are very difficult to live with.'

'And what is a romantic?' Karina asked.

'Someone who is always trying to matchmake in one way or another,' Garland said. 'They cannot bear to see an unattached man or an unattached woman. They just have to link them up together somehow. As a matter of fact Sadie's tried it before, but I've got a special sales resistance to that lady's ideas.'

Karina sipped the champagne. Perhaps it was the good dinner she had enjoyed and the excellent wine which gave her the courage to say:

'You sound very fierce and frightening. Is that how you manage to keep all the lovely ladies at bay?'

For a moment Garland glared at her as if he thought she had been impertinent, and then he laughed.

'You're incorrigible,' he said. 'And, what's more, you make me feel rather a fool. One thing, you have made your feelings quite clear. When I walked into my grandmother's room and heard you say that I was the last man on earth that you would marry, I really felt quite piqued.'

'You can't expect every woman to admire you as much as Sadie Westenholtz does,' Karina said demurely.

'Does she admire me?' he enquired.

'Enormously,' Karina answered solemnly. 'She thinks you are reserved, stiff-lipped and exactly like a movie star.'

Garland threw back his head again. He looked much younger Karina thought, when he laughed. In fact he looked his right age. It was only when he was glowering and being difficult that he seemed so very much older, so stern and so frightening.

'I tell you what, Karina,' he said, leaning forward.

She bent towards him. At that moment there was an interruption.

'A telephone call for Miss Karina Burke,' a page-boy said at her elbow.

'For me?' Karina said. 'There must be some mistake.'

'Miss Karina Burke wanted on the telephone,' the boy replied.

'I can't think who it can be,' she said.

'Better go and find out,' he suggested.

He sat back in his chair and put his cigar to his lips. Karina rose from the table. The boy led her up into the front hall of the hotel and showed her into a telephone-box. She lifted the receiver.

'Karina Burke speaking,' she said.

'One moment, I have a call for you,' the operator replied.

Who could it be? Karina wondered. Had Uncle Simon or Aunt Margaret found out where she was? Was it Felix ringing her? If it was, there must be something very wrong. She held her breath as she heard a click and the operator said:

'You're through.'

'Hello!' Her voice trembled so that she hardly recognised it as her own.

'Hello, Karina!'

It was Jim.

'Jim!' she exclaimed. 'Why are you telephoning me?'

'I wanted to find out how you are getting on. Is the great man in a good or a bad temper?'

'Jim, you ought not to have rung me.'

'Why not? He ruined my evening, didn't he? I'm only going to take up a few minutes of your time. I thought I was entitled to that, at least.'

'Oh, Jim, he won't like it and he'll ask me who wanted me.'

'Tell the truth and shame the devil.'

'I can't. You know he'll be cross.'

'What's it matter if he is? If you get the sack, I'll find you a job.'

'Selling cars?' Karina asked.

'No, looking after me.'

'Oh, Jim. I can't stay here talking. I must go back.'

'Actually I rang you up for a very important reason. There's something I had to tell you.'

'What is it?' Karina asked apprehensively.

'I wanted to tell you that I love you. I think you are the prettiest, most adorable girl I have ever seen.'

'You are absurd and I don't believe a word of it.'

'Yes, you do, and I'm going to make you believe it even more tomorrow night. Are you looking forward to coming out with me?'

'Yes, yes, of course.'

'Well, that's all I wanted to hear. I love you, Karina, and I can't wait to see you again. In fact I'm hating every minute of this evening because I am not with you.'

There was a sudden depth of feeling in Jim's voice.

'Thank you, Jim, but I mustn't stop. I must go, really.'

'All right. Good night! Bless you! Don't forget about me.'

'No; good night!'

Karina put down the receiver and for a moment she did not go from the box. Instead she put her fingers up to her lips –

the lips that Jim had kissed only a very short time ago. There had been so much to think about that until now she had forgotten that quick, snatched kiss – the first she had ever known in her whole life.

'He's nice,' she thought. 'Very nice.' And yet somehow there was something wrong. She didn't know what it was. And then she admitted to herself that it was disappointment. She had thought a kiss would be somehow different. More wonderful; perhaps more exciting. 'Perhaps it will be better the second time,' she told herself, and felt herself blush because she was certain that wasn't the sort of thing a nice girl ought to think.

She left the telephone-box and went slowly back to the table in the restaurant. Garland was still sitting there alone. Sadie and Carl Westenholtz, locked in each other's arms, were dancing cheek to cheek, oblivious to everyone and everything else.

Karina sat down. Somehow she didn't dare to look at Garland. He rose perfunctorily as she seated herself and, bending across the table, filled up her glass with champagne.

'Well?' he said.

'Well what?' Karina asked.

'Who was it?'

She felt a little frightened, but she forced a smile to her lips.

'Are you asking me as my employer or as a friend?'

'I'm asking you because I am curious,' Garland replied.

'I had an old nanny once who always used to say "Curiosity killed the cat!"' Karina said frivolously.

Garland was obviously not amused.

'I want to know.'

'But why?' Karina asked. 'It was nothing to do with business, I can assure you of that.'

'Was it likely to be?' he asked. Then almost angrily he said: 'Stop prevaricating and provoking me. Why shouldn't you say who telephoned you?'

'I think,' Karina answered slowly, 'because I am independent-minded. I don't like being ordered about or bullied.'

'Dammit all! I'm not bullying you,' Garland said. 'I asked you a perfectly simple question. Who telephoned you.'

'I'll give you a perfectly simple answer,' Karina said. 'It was a friend.'

'I'm almost certain who that friend was,' Garland answered.

He spoke quite angrily, and Karina said apprehensively:

'Don't make a row. It's so embarrassing.'

'A row!' he repeated. 'I'm not making a row or anything else. I'm just asking a simple question, and for some infuriating, aggravating, stupid reason you won't give me a simple answer. Don't worry, I know. It was Jim – and he's doing this just to annoy me.'

Karina said nothing. She looked down at the table, and then at that moment, to her relief, the Westenholtzes returned. There was no question of any more intimate conversation. Sadie held the table and talked and talked until Karina began to feel there was nothing else left in the world for anyone to say.

The cabaret kept her quiet for a little while and then, when it was finished, Garland called for the bill.

'Carl and I are hoping very much that you will come and see us while we're in London,' Sadie said to Karina. 'We shall be at the Ritz for a week and we'd both appreciate it if you would dine with us next week.'

'It's very kind of you to ask me,' Karina said.

'It will be kind of you to come,' Sadie answered. 'Just write down your address and telephone number.'

'Well, you can get me during the day at Mr Holt's office,' Karina said.

'Then that's just fine,' Sadie said. 'Carl has that in his little notebook, haven't you, honey?'

'I have,' Carl Westenholtz replied.

'That's settled then,' Sadie smiled, rising to her feet. 'I'll give you a ring and we'll fix

up a real gay party. Maybe just the four of us
– or perhaps one or two of my special
friends who are over here too.'

Chattering, she walked beside Karina to
the cloakroom, where they collected their
wraps.

'If you ask me, he's going to be just crazy
about you,' Sadie said as she put a white
mink stole around her shoulders.

'Who?' Karina asked.

'Garland Holt, of course,' Sadie replied. 'I
feel it in my bones that he will be popping
the question before you know where you
are.'

'Oh no, you're quite wrong,' Karina said.
'As a matter of fact he's very annoyed with
me at the moment.'

'Don't you take any notice of that,' Sadie
admonished her. 'Carl and I will do everything to bring you together and then you'll
be just as happy as we are.'

Karina felt she couldn't argue any longer,
so she just smiled sweetly, thanked the
American girl and made a mental reservation that it would be best if she didn't go
to the party.

The men were waiting for them in the hall.
As the women reached them, Carl Westenholtz looked at his watch.

'It's not yet one o'clock,' he said. 'What
about going on to a nightclub?'

'Thank you very much, but I must go

206

home,' Karina replied. 'I'm not used to such late nights; and I have to work in the morning.'

She saw the relief on Garland's face and knew that he had had enough of the Americans.

'Good night, Carl,' he said. 'I'll give you a ring tomorrow about those matters we discussed, and you might take a look at the legal aspect.'

'O.K!' Carl replied.

Sadie kissed Karina and said several times over again that she intended to ask her to a party. Then at last they had driven away in a taxi and Garland helped Karina into the car. He did not speak, and after he had put a big fur rug over her knees she wondered if he was still angry.

The car turned out of the Savoy yard into the Strand. There was not much traffic at this time of night and it moved swiftly. They had reached Trafalgar Square before Karina said in a small voice:

'Thank you for taking me out this evening. I have enjoyed it very much.'

'Carl Westenholtz is a very clever man,' Garland said in a conversational tone. 'His wife is a bore.'

'She was very kind to me,' Karina said, feeling somehow that she must defend Sadie from his condemnation of her.

'Nevertheless she was a bore,' Garland

said. 'No woman should be allowed to talk as much as that.'

'Perhaps her husband hasn't got such autocratic ideas as you,' Karina said a little shyly.

'I'm not so autocratic as you try to make out,' Garland retorted.

Karina couldn't think of an answer to this and so she said nothing. The car moved on into Piccadilly, turning up Park Lane towards Marble Arch.

'I shall have to get out soon,' Karina thought. 'I wish the evening hadn't ended like this.' She knew that there was a barrier between them, a coldness which seemed almost tangible in the atmosphere.

The car drove on. Karina looked out of the window beside her, but all the time she was very conscious of Garland sitting still in his corner of the car, staring straight ahead.

They reached the narrow street where the Carters' house was. The chauffeur had difficulty in finding it and they finally drew up on the wrong side a little way down the road.

'I can't see the numbers, sir,' he said to Garland. 'I'll get out and look for number twenty-five.'

'No, no, it's quite all right,' Karina said quickly. 'I know where it is.'

She pushed aside the rug and stepped out into the street before Garland could say anything. Then, as she turned to say good night, she found he was beside her.

'Don't bother to come with me,' she said quickly. 'It's only a very short distance.'

'I'll walk with you,' he said in that determined and final tone to which she knew there was no argument.

She pulled her velvet wrap around her shoulders because there was a touch of frost in the air and they walked back down the empty street and across the road. There were not many street lamps and Karina had to look carefully before she was quite certain which house was number twenty-five. It had a small stone portico over the door which cast a shadow and made it difficult to read the numbers.

She stopped at the bottom of the steps.

'Good night!' she said a little nervously. 'And thank you again.'

'Give me your key,' Garland replied. 'I'll open the door for you.'

He walked up the steps and she followed him, taking her key from the little velvet bag which matched her wrap. He took the key from her and fitted it in the lock. The door opened easily. He turned to hold out his hand.

'Good night, Karina!'

'Good night,' she answered. 'Thank you very much for this evening.'

There was a moment's pause while he still

held her hand, and then she said impulsively:

'Please don't be angry. I'm sorry if I upset you.'

She felt his fingers tighten on hers before he released them.

'It wasn't your fault.'

'But it was,' she agreed. 'I should have told you at once and not made a mystery of it. I … I was only teasing.'

He stood looking down at her. The distant lights glittering on the silver on her dress seemed to be reflected in her eyes.

'You must take advice sometimes,' he said harshly.

'I shall be all right,' she said with a smile. 'I can look after myself.'

'Not where Jim is concerned,' Garland replied.

Karina turned towards the door.

'Please don't let's discuss it again,' she pleaded almost piteously. 'It only makes you angry.'

She would have gone in, but Garland put a restraining hand on her arm.

'You've only just met Jim,' he said. 'Why do you stand up for him? I want you to believe me when I tell you that he's no good. Can you really have fallen in love with him so quickly?'

'No, no, of course I haven't.'

'But he's made love to you, hasn't he?'

'You've got no right to ask that sort of question,' Karina said quickly.

'But he has, hasn't he?' Garland insisted. 'You wouldn't answer me before, but you shall answer this. Jim has made love to you as he makes love to every woman he meets. I know he has!'

'Then why ask me if you know the answer?' Karina retorted with a flash of temper.

'You little fool!' Garland said scornfully. 'Do you really think that you can listen to what a man like that says to you? Can you really believe a word he says?'

'I'm not saying I believe him or I don't believe him,' Karina replied. 'I only say you have no right to ask such questions, to make such insinuations.'

'There you are, sticking up for him again,' Garland said angrily. 'He's got you hypnotised, I suppose. The poor, stupid, innocent little fly from the country who walked into the web that's been nicely spun for her by a town spider! Oh, Karina, do have some sense! You can't be so stupid as all that.'

'Please, Mr Holt, I don't want to discuss this any further,' Karina said. 'You employ me, and while I am in the office I will do my best to serve you and to do everything you ask. But what I do outside is my own business, just as my friends – the few I have got – are my business, too.'

211

She tried to move away from his restraining hand, but he tightened his hold on her arm.

'I'm not going to let you go like that,' he said. 'I took you out to dinner to get you away from Jim, and yet you had him here before I picked you up. I thought I recognised him in a car driving down the street. He was here, wasn't he?'

'All right, he was,' Karina replied defiantly. 'There's nothing wrong in that, is there?'

'It depends what you mean by wrong,' Garland said slowly.

He stood looking at her as if he was remembering something.

'Jim had just left you when I arrived,' he said slowly, 'and when I came into the room you were standing with a flush on your cheeks, your eyes shining – and your fingers were touching your mouth.'

He spoke as if he was seeing a picture and describing it; and then suddenly his fingers bit cruelly into her arm as he said:

'He'd kissed you, hadn't he? He kissed you just before I arrived.'

'I won't listen to you, I won't!' Karina stormed. 'Let me go.'

She tried to tear herself free, but Garland's grasp was like a band of steel.

'He kissed you,' he said again accusingly. 'You stupid little idiot. If it's kisses you wanted, why take Jim's?'

And then, before Karina realised what was happening, before she could cry out or tear herself free of him, his arms were round her. He crushed her to him roughly and his lips found hers.

He kissed her brutally with a violence which seemed to force the very life from between her lips. She wanted to gasp for air, but his arms held her closer and closer. She felt her lips quiver beneath his, she felt as if his mouth conquered her, possessing her utterly, so that she had no longer any identity of her own but was a part of him.

And then as suddenly and unexpectedly as he had taken her, he set her free. He thrust her from him so that she staggered against the open doorway. He turned and walked down the steps and out into the street.

She couldn't see him go, she couldn't think. She could only feel that burning, passionate, possessive kiss upon her lips – a kiss which seemed to have seared its way right into her very soul.

CHAPTER NINE

'How dare he! How dare he!'

Karina found herself muttering the words over and over again as she tossed from side to side, unable to sleep. And yet, at the same time, she was not really angry; only bewildered, astonished and, within herself, upset in a way she could not explain.

She tried to sort out in her mind the tangled relationship between Garland and his cousin Jim; and, though she tried to avoid it, her own relationship with Garland Holt.

Because there didn't seem an answer to any of the questions that she posed to herself, she rose soon after dawn and started to dress.

It was then that she realised that she would have to meet Garland again at the office, and the colour came flooding into her cheeks at the very thought. How could she face him? How could she speak to him when all night her lips had throbbed because of the violence of his kiss, because they still felt bruised and tender when she touched them with the tips of her fingers?

She had been kissed twice in the same day!

She looked at her reflection in the mirror and wondered if she would see any difference. But instead, a very young and rather frightened face looked back at her – the face of a child who doesn't understand the world she sees opening before her.

'I can't go to the office,' Karina thought in a panic. And then pride came to her rescue. Why should she run away? Why should she let Garland Holt think that his unforgivable action had disturbed or upset her in any way? It was up to him to apologise, up to him to say he was sorry for what was an inexcusable act.

Slowly she finished dressing and then went to look out of the window. The pale March sun was glinting through the clouds, but there was a strong north wind which made people hug their coats around them and hurry by with blue noses.

'He is like the north wind,' Karina thought, and remembered that moment when he had come into the room and she had felt as if he was propelled by some dynamic force.

'I won't be frightened of him, I won't,' she said aloud, and went down to breakfast with her head held high.

'You're very early, miss,' Mrs Carter said as she entered the kitchen.

'It's such a nice morning that I thought I might walk to work,' Karina said on the spur of the moment.

And when she had said it, she thought that perhaps the wind would blow away the cobwebs of the night before. Perhaps, too, it would blow away the embarrassment and shyness she felt throbbing beneath her heart, so that when Mrs Carter had set bacon and eggs in front of her she knew she could not eat a mouthful.

She drank her tea and nibbled a piece of toast. Every crumb seemed to stick in her throat. Resolutely, however, she went upstairs to get her hat and coat and put on her walking shoes.

'Goodbye, Mrs Carter!' she called as she opened the front door, then shut it behind her with a bang.

For a moment it seemed to her that she could see Garland Holt standing there, feel his arms suddenly reaching out towards her, feel herself breathless beneath his kiss... She almost ran down the road to escape from the ghosts of last night.

She was the first to reach the office. Beth came in a few minutes later and talked to her while she sorted her papers and put a new ribbon in her typewriter. Karina knew that Beth was full of curiosity over Jim, but somehow not even to be pleasant and friendly could she talk about Jim or any other man this morning. After trying vainly to coax her confidence, Beth gave up with a shrug of her shoulders.

'Westie's late this morning,' she said, looking at the clock. 'The hydrogen bomb must have arrived and we didn't know it.'

'Is she always on time?' Karina asked.

'On the stroke,' Beth said.

Karina finished inserting the new ribbon and, finding she had nothing to do, sat waiting, expecting Miss Weston to arrive at any moment.

Time went by. Ten o'clock came; half-past; and she was just wondering whether she ought to go into the outer office and see if there was anything that required doing when the door opened and Miss Weston came bustling in.

'Oh, there you are, Miss Burke,' she said unnecessarily, 'Will you come into the inner office, please. I have got something for you to do.'

She did not take off her hat and coat and Karina followed her, wondering what was the matter. Miss Weston opened a notebook on Garland Holt's desk.

'Take down the names of these appointments for the next week,' she said. 'They are all written quite clearly and you will find the addresses and telephone numbers in the book on my desk.'

Without waiting for Karina to reply she started manipulating the dial of a large safe in the wall. For a moment there was only the click-click of the turning lock and then the door opened and Miss Weston began to collect papers from inside the safe.

Automatically Karina copied the names on Garland Holt's engagement pad until at last her curiosity was too much for her. She must know what was happening. She had to ask the question.

'Is anything the matter?'

Miss Weston looked round in surprise.

'No, of course not. Mr Holt is leaving for India, that's all.'

'For India!'

Karina thought her voice sounded almost shrill in her astonishment.

'Yes, he had a cable this morning and decided to fly out right away. I shall be with him until he leaves, of course. Now, what I want you to do is to telephone all those people and say that Mr Holt will be away for a week but will get in touch with them immediately on his return. Is that clear?'

'Yes,' Karina said, 'quite clear.'

She took her notebook into the outer office and, picking up Miss Weston's address book, sat down at her own desk. But somehow she could not find the numbers she sought. They seemed to swim before her eyes. She could think of only one thing – Garland was going away. He was going to India and she would not see him today.

She felt suddenly flat, as if all the energy

and spirit had been taken from her body. She had been keyed up to meet him, buoyed up by her pride and her determination not to run away. And now it was all unnecessary.

Miss Weston came out of the inner office, closed the door and said:

'Get through to those people as soon as you can. If you can't speak to them personally, speak to their private secretaries and say, of course, that Mr Holt regrets very much to postpone his engagement. There's no need for me to tell you that.'

'No, of course not,' Karina murmured.

But Miss Weston had not waited to hear her reply. She had gone and Karina was alone in the office. She sat for some moments staring ahead of her. She was conscious of feeling strange in some manner that she had never felt before. Then, with an effort, she picked up the telephone and began her task of working through the names on her list.

It took her over an hour and she had just finished when the telephone rang. She picked it up.

'Good morning, my dear!'

'Oh, it's you, Cousin Felix.'

'Whom did you expect?'

'Nobody. I was just surprised when I recognised your voice.'

'Will you come and lunch with me today? I want to talk to you.'

'Thank you, I'd like to very much.'

Even as she spoke she knew that she didn't really want to lunch with Cousin Felix, and then chid herself for being ungrateful and ridiculous.

'I'll pick you up at one o'clock.'

'Thank you.'

There seemed to be nothing else for her to do now that Miss Weston had gone, and she was waiting on the steps downstairs when Felix drove up in a taxi.

'Cars are too much of a nuisance in these crowded streets,' he said. 'Come along, I have booked a table in a new place which has just opened. I'm told the food is delicious.'

The restaurant was only a few minutes' drive from the office and as they went Karina thanked Felix for the dress and told him who they had dined with the night before. After they had arrived and Felix had ordered what seemed to Karina a very large meal, he leant back against the red plush sofa and said:

'Now tell me about the office. How are you getting on?'

'I haven't had very much to do yet,' Karina said. 'And this morning everything was upset because Mr Holt is going to India.'

'To India?' Felix enquired almost sharply.

Karina nodded.

'Yes, it was quite unexpected. Miss Weston

arrived late and said he had received a cable which necessitated him flying out this afternoon. So the only thing I had to do was to put off all his appointments for next week.'

Felix didn't answer for a moment and then he said:

'There must have been quite a number of them.'

'It took me over an hour.'

'And who were they?'

Karina was just going to tell him when suddenly she stopped. Surely, she thought, it was a breach of confidence to relate details of your employer's engagements to someone outside the firm.

'Oh, they were just business people,' she said vaguely.

'Of course, but what business people?' Felix enquired. 'I'm interested.'

There was something in the way he spoke, although his words were light enough, that made Karina feel quite certain that he was really anxious to know the answer to his question. She felt her heart give a little frightened throb as she answered:

'I don't think, Cousin Felix, that I ought to tell you that.'

'Why not?'

She had not expected him to challenge her and she answered, faltering a little:

'Well, I ... I was doing something which ... only concerned Mr Holt and Miss Weston, his private secretary...' Her voice tailed away.

Felix was looking at her in a manner which seemed to take the very words from her lips.

'Listen, Karina,' he said, and his voice was smooth and low but with steel beneath it. 'You and I are in this together. I have helped you in a dangerous and difficult moment of your life. Had I not come to Letchfield Park, have you thought what you would be doing at this moment?' He paused to let his words sink in and then he said: 'You would be married to your cousin Cyril – a man who is mental! A marriage which would certainly not have brought you happiness but only revulsion and horror.'

'Yes, yes, I know,' Karina said quickly, 'and I am grateful, you know I'm grateful.'

'Then I am suggesting that you should prove your gratitude,' Felix went on, 'by not arguing with me when I ask you a trivial and ordinary question. There is nothing fundamentally wrong in telling me with whom Garland would be lunching and dining this next week. Indeed, I'm sure he would be the last person to keep it a secret. But I am interested in what would have been his movements, and I wish you to tell me exactly whom you telephoned to this morning.'

Karina felt almost faint. This was wrong! She knew it was wrong, and yet how could

223

she refuse to answer Felix? And then before she could reply he went on:

'Have you forgotten, my dear, that you are not yet twenty-one? If you regret my knight-errantry, if you prefer to return home, then I am sure you will find Cyril waiting for you with open arms.'

It was a threat and Karina knew it.

'Please, Cousin Felix! Please don't frighten me. It is quite unnecessary. I will tell you what you want to know.'

'Good!'

There was a glint of triumph in Felix's eyes, but there was, too, a cruel twist at the corners of his mouth as if in some way he enjoyed torturing her. He took a beautifully chased gold pencil from his pocket and a neat, leather notebook with gold edges.

Slowly he took down the names, one by one, while Karina felt with every one she uttered that she was soiled and tarnished.

'Is that all?' Felix asked.

'That is all,' she answered.

'Thank you, my dear. Don't look so tragic about it. You have not betrayed the secrets of the nation of a foreign power. You have only told me what Garland himself would have told me had I asked him.'

Karina doubted this, but there was nothing she could say. Miserably she drank her coffee and, glancing at her watch, said it was time for her to return to the office.

'Thank you for my lunch,' she said to Felix.

He made no offer to take her back, but watched her walk away while he stood on the steps of the restaurant waiting for a taxi.

Alone in the office, Karina saw the list of names lying on her desk and wondered why she had felt so guilty in giving them to Felix. After all, as he had said, there was nothing particularly secret about them. There was no reason why Garland shouldn't lunch with a businessman without it involving in any way high finance or special secret negotiations.

Why, why, should she feel so upset? Why did she know instinctively that something was wrong? Restlessly, and because she had nothing to do, she got up and opened the door of the inner office and went in.

It was furnished very simply with a grey carpet, deep maroon-coloured chairs and grey curtains over wide, modern windows. There was nothing very individual, nothing very distinctive about it, and yet it seemed to Karina in that moment to be redolent with the dynamic personality of Garland Holt.

It was then, as she stood there in the door, seeming to see him seated at the desk, his hand stretching out towards the telephone, that she knew that she loved him. It came to her in a sudden flash almost like a clap of thunder. She felt, too, as if a streak of lightning passed through her body, making her quiver and tremble so that she went forward a few steps to hold blindly on to the back of a chair.

She loved him! It wasn't possible. It was incredible, absurd, ridiculous – and yet she knew it was the truth! She knew now why the hard pressure of his lips was still on hers; why all day she had felt her heart beating strangely and in a turbulent manner beneath her breast; why the thought that she would not see him had sent her suddenly into the depths of despair.

'I love him! I love him!'

She said it aloud and hoped it was not true, but her body quivered and she knew it was, indeed, the truth. She must have loved him even while she had been protesting to his grandmother that he was the last man in the world she would marry. She must have loved him when he carried her up the stairs to her bedroom and she had felt safe and secure because of his strength and the hard pressure of his arms.

She had loved him while she defied him. She had loved him even while she hated him. It was mad, crazy, ridiculous! she told herself, and then knew that nothing altered the fact that she still loved him.

And now, in her love, she knew why she had resented Felix's curiosity. It was for fear that Felix with his hard, cruel lips and shrewd eyes, would hurt Garland.

It was a ridiculous thought. How could anyone hurt the great, all-conquering, invincible Garland Holt? And yet, because of her love, she wanted to protect him.

'I must go away,' Karina said to herself. 'If I stay here I shall make a fool of myself.'

She thought of all the other women who had loved Garland and from whom he had fled, sneering at them, laughing at them, all to conscious that they pursued him. Karina vowed she would never be like one of them.

She could see Lady Carol, with her beautiful, much-photographed face and exquisite, expensive clothes. If Garland did not love her, was it likely he would be interested in a rather boring little typist who had been foisted on him by a man he didn't like?

Karina gave a little sob because it was all so hopeless – to love a man who was pursued by every woman in the land because he was so rich and who had already made it quite clear that he was interested in none of them. And yet, she thought, he had asked her out last night. That, of course, was to spite Jim, who, for some reason, had incurred his anger.

But he had kissed her good night. For a moment she shut her eyes, feeling again that kiss, that rough, possessive, passionate kiss which had left her breathless and shaky.

She knew now that her love for him, smouldering secretly within her, had burst into flame the very moment that he had touched her. She knew now that the sudden arrow which had seemed to pierce her had been, in fact, an awakening to the realisation of her love although she had not known it at the time.

All night long she had lain awake trying to feel angry, trying to feel incensed at what had occurred; and all the time denying the truth.

'I love him! I love him!'

She went across to the window and rested her head against the softness of the curtains. The sunshine was on her eyes, blinding them. She was glad of it. She didn't want to see anything but Garland's face, Garland's smile, Garland looking angry, Garland being sarcastic and sneering; Garland bitter and vindictive, Garland being gentle, kind and understanding.

At his best or at his worst she still loved him.

How long she stood there she had no idea. Time must have gone by on silent feet, for she suddenly awoke to the fact that the sun had disappeared behind the clouds and the early darkness was beginning to seep into the streets.

It was then that the door opened and Beth said:

'Miss Weston wants to speak to you. Didn't you hear your telephone ring?'

Karina came back to reality from a world which contained only Garland Holt.

'N-no, no, I'm a-afraid I didn't,' she stammered.

'Well, you must be deaf,' Beth said cheerily. 'You'd better speak to her, and hurry, she'll be in an awful bat otherwise.'

Karina ran to her own desk and picked up the telephone.

'Is that you, Miss Burke?' Miss Weston's voice asked. 'Where have you been?'

'I'm so sorry,' Karina said. 'I was tidying some papers.'

'Well, I rang to tell you that I'm not coming back to the office this afternoon. I have just seen Mr Holt off and I can do what he wants done today at home, so if you've nothing to do you can get off early. We shall very likely have to work late tomorrow.'

'Thank you, Miss Weston.'

She was trying to take in what Miss Weston was telling her, but all the time she was conscious of only one bit of information – Garland was gone. She imagined him flying away in the Comet, up into the skies, away from England – away from her!

'Please be punctual in the morning,' Miss Weston was saying.

'Yes, of course,' Karina replied.

The line went dead. Automatically she covered her typewriter and, putting on her hat and coat, went from the office with only a brief word of farewell to Beth. She took a bus part of the way and walked the rest, but all the time she was hardly conscious of the people around her, jostling, hurrying, struggling to get home. She was lost in her own thoughts, in her own feelings.

She was just passing through one of the larger squares north of Marble Arch when suddenly she heard an exclamation and her name called.

'Karina!'

'Awakening from her reverie, she turned her head and saw with a sudden sense of panic that, blindly engrossed in her own thoughts, she had walked slap into Uncle Simon!

He was standing there, looking, she thought, extraordinarily fierce, his bushy eyebrows bristling under his bowler hat, his rolled umbrella held almost like a weapon.

'Karina,' he said again, and the very name seemed to her an accusation. 'You nearly bumped into me.'

'I'm ... I'm sorry,' she said, her eyes wide with fright, wondering whether she should run or stay.

'Well, it's dangerous to go about like that,' Uncle Simon said. 'You might get run over.'

'Yes ... yes, I know,' Karina said.

'Well, how are you getting on?'

She stared at him in utter astonishment. She had expected many things but not this.

'Getting on?' she echoed, feeling almost like a village idiot as she repeated his words.

'Yes, Felix told us that he had got you a job in an office. How do you like it?'

'Felix told you?'

Karina could hardly get the words out.

'Yes, yes, of course,' Uncle Simon said testily. He had always disliked people who were slow-brained. 'Felix told us that you were with … er … er … Holt – yes, that was the name. I've heard of him, of course. Is he a decent sort of chap?'

'Yes, q-quite decent.'

'Good, and you like the work? Your Aunt Margaret was convinced you'd want to give it up at the end of a week.'

'No, I … I like it very much,' Karina stammered.

'That's good,' Uncle Simon remarked.

He seemed to hesitate and suddenly, to Karina's surprise, she realised that he was embarrassed.

'Glad you're all right,' he said at length a little gruffly. 'Sorry you had to take the bit between your teeth and bolt as you did. Had no idea until you'd gone that you didn't want to marry the boy. Dare say we took too much for granted, eh?'

He was making an apology. Karina knew

231

that and impulsively she put out her hands towards him.

'Oh, Uncle Simon, you're not angry?'

'Angry? Of course not,' he said quickly. 'Taken aback when you disappeared! When Felix explained things, we realised you were too young! Hadn't seen enough of the world. Well, let us know how you get on. Your aunt would appreciate a letter from you now and again.'

As if he felt that he had said too much, or perhaps too little, he raised his hat and stumbled off down the road, leaving her staring after him, hardly able to comprehend what he had said.

Felix had told them all the time! They hadn't been looking for her. She need not have been afraid. Yet only today at lunch... She could see Felix's eyes and the sharp line of his mouth as he threatened her. She could hear her own voice saying:

'Please, Cousin Felix, please don't frighten me.'

Uncle Simon was almost out of sight. She had an impulse to run after him, to tell him just how treacherous Cousin Felix had been. And then she checked herself. If she said too much, he would obviously press her to return home. That was one thing she could never do. She couldn't face Cyril again and she had the feeling that Aunt Margaret might not be as amenable as

Uncle Simon.

But why the lies? Why the continual hints and innuendoes that she must be careful, that she must keep out of sight, that she was not yet twenty-one? What was Felix doing? What was his point in behaving in this extraordinary way?

She walked home, bemused and worried, to hear Mrs Carter calling her even as she opened the door.

'Is that you, Miss Burke? There's a gentleman rung up three times. He said that he missed you at the office.'

'What's his name?' Karina asked.

'Mr Holt.'

Just for a moment her heart gave a silly jump, and then she knew it was Jim who had called her, just as she had expected he would.

'His number's on the pad by the telephone,' Mrs Carter shouted.

'I've found it, thank you,' Karina replied.

She stood looking at the number. She had promised to go out with Jim tonight. She had forgotten all about it because she had been so intent on her thoughts of another Mr Holt.

Quite suddenly she decided she would not go. She wanted to be alone; she wanted to think; she wanted to go on remembering every moment when she had been alone with Garland, every word he had said to her.

She stood still, staring at the number; and then she knew that if she rang Jim up he would persuade her to meet him. She walked into the kitchen.

'Mrs Carter,' she said. 'I wonder if you would be very kind and do something for me? I've got a headache and I want to lie down on my bed. Would you ring Mr Holt and say I can't come out with him tonight?'

'He'll be upset if you don't,' Mrs Carter said. 'Ringing up in a terrible flap he was because he'd missed you at the office. "Tell her to ring me the moment she gets in," he says.'

'I can't help it,' Karina replied. 'I don't want to go out with him.'

'There's no reason why you should if you don't want to,' Mrs Carter remarked. 'Not that he didn't sound a nice young man to me. Polite and pleasant – different to the way some of them talk on the telephone these days.'

'Put him off for me, Mrs Carter, there's a dear,' Karina begged.

She went towards the door, but Mrs Carter's voice stopped her.

'Is there anything the matter, Miss Burke? You look upset.'

'No, not really,' Karina answered.

'Is there any way I can help you, miss?' Mrs Carter enquired.

Karina shook her head.

'No, it's very kind of you, but nobody can help.'

'If it's as bad as that, it sounds as if you're in love,' Mrs Carter said jokingly.

Karina did not reply, but as she went up the stairs her footsteps seemed to echo the words:

'You're in love! In love! In love!'

CHAPTER TEN

To Karina's surprise, when she went to bed she slept. She thought she would stay awake hugging to herself the new-found knowledge of her love or questioning Cousin Felix's strange and unaccountable behaviour.

But instead she fell into a troubled sleep in which her dreams chased one another in wild, chaotic confusion, and she awoke with a start to hear her own voice, sharp with terror, crying: 'Don't hurt him! Don't hurt him!'

She opened her eyes and found the pale morning sun seeping through the sides of the curtains and she knew that in her dream she had been afraid for Garland – afraid that Felix might injure him.

'I am being ridiculous,' she told herself severely. 'How could Felix hurt anyone so rich, so powerful as Garland Holt?'

She tried to laugh away her fears, remembering Felix's somewhat dilettante manner, his elegant little bachelor flat, and comparing it with the vast possessions, great fortune and the powerful City interests of Garland. Unfortunately the comparison did not disparage Felix, but only herself.

Who was she, she wondered, an insignificant, unsophisticated girl from the country, to raise her eyes towards anyone so important as Garland Holt?

She drew back the curtains and in her nightgown walked across the room towards the dressing-table. As she did so, she felt the linoleum chill against her feet and saw, as if it were in a picture, the general shabbiness of Mrs Carter's back bedroom.

She had a sudden vision of the comfort and luxury of Garland Holt's home. Then, even as it struck her almost like a blow, she saw her own reflection in the mirror and laughed aloud. She looked like a child – a child with fair hair in a white dress; a child who knew nothing of the world but just lived in a fantasy world of its own.

'I've got to forget him,' Karina said aloud.

But even as she spoke the words, her heart throbbed with the intensity of her love for him. She loved his clear-cut features, she thought; the way his eyebrows almost met across his nose when he frowned; the little twinkle in the depths of his eyes when he was being deliberately provocative; the way in which his smile would suddenly flash out when one least expected it.

Did Lady Carol feel like this? Karina asked herself, and knew the bitterness and hurt that jealousy can bring.

She dressed slowly and went downstairs to find Mrs Carter full of Jim and how upset he had been by her message the night before.

'He sounded real concerned about you,' she said. 'It's a pity you had to give him the go-by. A nice young man he seemed to me.'

'Perhaps he will ask me again,' Karina said without any real enthusiasm.

'He will, indeed! He told me to tell you he would expect you to lunch with him today to make up for last night – and he wasn't going to take no for an answer.'

'Oh dear!' Karina exclaimed, but she smiled at the same time.

Somehow it was comforting to think someone wanted her, and she thought now how absurd she had been not to go out with Jim last night. What had been the point of brooding over Cousin Felix's perfidy or yearning for someone far away in India who would doubtless never give her a thought?

Jim was there on the spot. He was warm and human and kind, whatever Garland might say about him, and she had a sudden longing for someone to be kind to her.

She finished her breakfast, and Mrs Carter said:

'You don't eat enough to keep a flea alive. It's daylight robbery to take the money you pay me, it is, indeed!'

'I'm not hungry,' Karina said.

239

'Well, you'll get a good lunch at any rate,' Mrs Carter retorted. 'And don't be too unkind to that young man. It seems to me he's the genuine sort.'

Karina waved goodbye but said nothing. Jim would be complimented at being thought genuine, she thought, although she was quite certain that Garland would not agree with the description.

It was a cold morning, but the sun was shining and she walked quite a long way before she took a bus. Even so, she was early at the office and had time to sit down and think before the others arrived.

She decided she would write to Cousin Felix and ask him why he had deliberately lied to her about Uncle Simon and Aunt Margaret. It was too difficult to face him with it. Besides, she wasn't brave enough. And then with a sudden start she realised that she was free – free of Cousin Felix and his threats, free really of her gratitude.

He had used her cleverly, she could see that. But why he should have done so she could not understand. Could it really matter to him whom Garland lunched with? Had it really been to get information of that sort that he had manoeuvred to get her into the office?

She pulled a piece of writing-paper in front of her, picked up her pen and put it down again. She would draft out a letter in pencil first, she thought, and then copy it out.

She began: *'Dear Cousin Felix...'* then stopped.

What could she say to him? How hard to put her suspicions into words, and harder still to accuse him of deliberately misleading and misinforming her.

The telephone rang. The girl on the private exchange said:

'Is Miss Weston there?'

'No,' Karina answered. 'She hasn't come in yet.'

'It's unlike her to be late,' the girl said. 'There's a cable here for her from Mr Holt.'

'Shall I take it down?' Karina asked. 'Then it will be ready when she arrives.'

'Very well,' the girl replied, and Karina took down at her dictation.

When she had finished, the girl said:

'Have you got that?'

'Yes, thank you,' Karina answered.

'It's only just arrived,' the girl said. 'So put the time on it. Miss Weston gets awfully batty if we don't send cables and telegrams through the moment they arrive.'

'All right,' Karina said. 'I'll make it nine-twenty.'

She glanced at the clock as she spoke and wondered again what had happened to Miss Weston. The cable was from Garland and, dull and authoritative though it was, it seemed to bring a little warm glow of happiness to her even to read it.

'Send notebook in safe stop Holt stop'

Nothing could be more prosaic, more matter-of-fact, Karina thought. And yet somehow it was a message from him from the other side of the world. She wondered what he had been doing when he wrote it. She wondered if he thought of them all sitting in the office receiving his instructions, hurrying to carry them out.

Then, trying to laugh at herself, she thought more than likely he had barked the order at some wretched secretary who had hurried away, even as she and Miss Weston would, to do his bidding like slaves attending to the commands of a Maharajah.

The telephone rang again and she put out her hand towards it.

'Is that Miss Burke?' a voice enquired.

'Yes, who is it?' Karina asked.

'It's Clare Weston speaking.'

'Oh, Miss Weston, I was just wondering where you were.'

'I'm ill. I am afraid I cannot get to the office today.'

'Oh, I am sorry!' Karina exclaimed.

'It must have been something I ate,' Miss Weston explained. 'I've never been taken like this before. I have been sick all night and simply daren't leave the house, not even for a moment.'

'But you mustn't think of doing anything

of the sort,' Karina said. 'Just lie down. Have you sent for the doctor?'

'No, I think the worst of it is over by now,' Miss Weston said. 'I hate making a fuss about myself. It's so unlike me to be ill, and it couldn't be at a worse moment with Mr Holt away.'

'Well, there don't seem to be any messages,' Karina said. 'Only a cable from Mr Holt.'

'A cable from Mr Holt!'

She heard Miss Weston's voice sharpen as she repeated the words.

'What does it say?'

'*Send notebook in safe,*' Karina read.

There was a moment's pause.

'Notebook in safe?' Miss Weston queried. 'I wonder what he means by that? There are several notebooks there. Are you quite sure that is all it says?'

'Quite sure,' Karina answered. 'But I'll ask the girl who took it if you like.'

'No, don't worry,' Miss Weston answered. 'Mr Holt will expect me to know. I shall have to come round somehow, though I don't know how I can manage it.'

As if the mere idea was too much for her, she gave a sudden gulp and said in an indistinct voice:

'Hold on ... for a ... moment.'

Karina could hear the telephone receiver being put down with a bang. She guessed that Miss Weston had gone away to be sick, and, taking up the other telephone, she spoke to the operator who had taken the cable.

'No,' the girl said. 'There was nothing else. Just *"Send notebook in safe"*. I expect he thought Miss Weston would know. She always knows everything.'

'Are there any other messages or calls for her?' Karina asked.

'Oh, a whole pile,' the operator said cheerfully. 'But Mavis has got those in the outer office. When Miss Weston's finished talking to you, you'd better let me switch her through, unless she's coming in.'

'She's ill,' Karina said.

'Good gracious!' the operator exclaimed. 'The sky must be falling down! I've been here five years and Miss Weston's never been ill all that time.'

Karina picked up the other receiver and waited. In about two or three minutes she heard Miss Weston's voice again, very faint and weak.

'I'm ... so ... sorry,' she said. 'I just ... can't do anything when ... these bouts of ... sickness come over me.'

'You must go back to bed,' Karina said.

'Mr Holt has ... got to have his ... notebook,' Miss Weston replied. 'Now, listen, Miss Burke, I've got to ... trust you. It's something I never ... imagined doing in my wildest dreams, but … I've got to do it. I will tell you … the combination of the safe.'

'Oh, isn't there anyone else?'

'Nobody,' Miss Weston said. 'As I think you know, Mr Holt's junior partners are both away. One is in Buenos Aires and the other in South Africa. That's why it's so maddening for me to be ill at this time.'

'Don't worry,' Karina said soothingly, hearing the agitation in Miss Weston's voice. 'Can't the notebook wait until tomorrow? You'll be all right by then.'

'If Mr Holt wants something, it has to be done at once,' Miss Weston replied. 'Now, it's not difficult. All you've got to do is to follow exactly the instructions I will give you. And then, when you have got the safe open, you can tell me what notebooks are there and I will tell you which one to send to him.'

'Very well,' Karina said.

She picked up a pencil and drew a block towards her. Miss Weston gave her the instructions. It was quite complicated; so many different numbers, so many turns of the lock.

'Now go and see if you can do it,' Miss Weston said, 'while I hold on.'

Karina heard the faintness in her voice and realised that she was near the end of her tether.

'Are you in bed?' she asked.

'No, the telephone is in the hall of my lodgings,' Miss Weston answered.

'Then go back to bed at once,' Karina said. 'If I can't manage it, I will ring you up, I promise you, and there can't be so many notebooks there, and what there are I will send him. It's no use killing yourself. You'll be no use to him dead.'

'I really ... don't think I can ... stand here much longer,' Miss Weston murmured.

'Then go back to bed at once,' Karina commanded.

'He will be ... in Delhi,' Miss Weston said weakly. 'They have ... the address in the outer office...'

The words tailed away in a sudden gulp and Karina knew Miss Weston was going to be sick again. She put down the receiver and, taking the piece of paper with the instructions on it, went into the inner office.

She looked at the safe rather apprehensively. It looked very strong and formidable and ready, she felt, to resist any onslaught she might make upon it. But Miss Weston's instructions were quite clear. She dialled the number, turned the handle of the lock the requisite number of times, there was a click and the door was open.

It was not a big safe and the papers were all extremely neatly arranged. On the top was a wad of typed papers clipped together and headed *'Holdings'*. Karina took it out and found underneath there were various legal-looking documents, and at the bottom, underneath them, two small note-books, one covered in green leather, the other in red.

She looked through the papers, but there were no other notebooks and, putting them on the desk, she replaced the other papers carefully. She had just lifted the ones marked *'Holdings'* from the table when the office door opened and someone came in. She turned her head and saw, to her astonishment, that it was Felix who had entered.

'Good morning, Karina!'

'Cousin Felix!' she exclaimed. 'What are you doing here?'

'I wanted to see you,' he answered. 'And they told me to come straight in.'

Summoning all her courage and her dignity, Karina said:

'Would you mind waiting for me outside? I am rather busy at the moment.'

Felix laughed.

'You sound very hoity-toity this morning. What's the matter, little cousin? Have I offended you?'

'Please wait a moment,' Karina repeated.

She pushed the papers she had in her hand quickly into the safe, pushed the heavy door to and was just going to turn the knob and lock it again when suddenly Felix seemed to fall against her, his whole weight sagging on to her shoulder so that she staggered to keep her feet.

'What ... what are you doing?' she ejaculated, only to realise that his eyes were closed and one of his hands was clutching at his collar.

Almost instinctively her arms went out to support him. She guided him to a chair, where he seemed to collapse.

'Water,' he murmured. 'Water.'

She looked wildly round the room, but as Garland was away there was no water on his desk. Karina wrenched open the door and ran through Miss Weston's office out to where the girls and clerks were busy working.

'Please, some water quickly,' she cried. 'Mr Mainwaring has been taken ill.'

It took a few seconds for someone to find a glass, fill it and bring it back.

'What is the matter with everyone this morning?' Karina thought agitatedly as she waited. 'First Miss Weston and now Cousin Felix.'

At length the glass, cold and rather wet on the outside, was thrust into her outstretched hand and she ran back into the inner office. Felix was still sitting on the chair where she had left him, but he seemed to have recovered.

He took the glass of water she held out to him, sipped it fastidiously, made a face and said:

'I'm sorry, my dear, if I gave you a fright. I get these attacks at times. It's my heart, you know.'

'Are you all right now?' Karina asked.

'Yes, they pass off. Actually I have some pills with me which I can swallow. You were so long with the water that I managed to get one down without assistance.'

'I'm so sorry,' Karina replied. 'It's always the same. When you want water it's never there.'

'I think perhaps I had better get home,' Felix said. 'I usually have to rest when I get a turn like this.'

'But of course,' Karina agreed. 'Let me help you to get a taxi.'

'That would be very kind of you,' Felix answered.

He got slowly to his feet, moving with difficulty, but dramatically, Karina thought, almost as if he were acting a part. And then she put the thought from her as being ungenerous. Felix leaned on her arm and she helped him through the outer office and into the lift. He sat down as they descended, his head bent.

Karina tried to feel sorry for him; at the same time she wished he was well enough so that she could face him with the news that she had seen Uncle Simon. But it was not a moment for recriminations or conversation.

In silence she helped him out of the lift, called to the doorman to get a taxi and waited until he was safely in it. She heard him give the address and she waved as he went away.

'I really couldn't say anything when he was ill,' she excused herself. She went back upstairs, and only when she reached her own office did she remember that she had not locked the safe.

She hurried through the door and saw that the two notebooks were lying on the desk where she had left them. She went to the safe, but the door was shut to and she was just about to turn the lock when she remembered that she had put the papers back in a hurry and wondered if they were untidy.

She opened the door again. For a moment she thought she must be dreaming. Then she knew all too clearly what had happened. The papers marked *'Holdings'* had gone!

For some moments she stood staring, believing that by some miracle she could have inadvertently put them at the bottom of the pile of papers. But she knew all the time it was only wishful thinking.

Slowly in her mind she went over exactly what had happened – Cousin Felix coming in through the door; the papers marked *'Holdings'* in her hand; the way she had put them hastily into the safe, turning her back on him; the manner in which he had lurched into her causing her to stagger, pulled at his tie, gasped out his cry for water! It was all too obvious. The whole thing had been an act.

She closed the safe door, locked it and tore into small pieces the instructions Miss Weston had given her for opening it. Then, picking up the notebooks, she went into her own office. She put on her coat and hat, and before going outside called the senior clerk and handed him the notebooks.

'Miss Weston says will you please post these immediately to Mr Holt?' she said. 'She's unable to come today as she's ill. I have got to go out. It's rather important. If she happens to ring and ask for me, will you say I shall be back shortly?'

'Very good, Miss Burke,' the clerk answered. 'I will send these at once.'

'Thank you,' Karina said.

She tried to smile but felt that her face was too stiff to permit movement of any sort. She hurried to the lift, willing it to go faster and yet faster so that she could reach the street in record time. She called the commissionaire to get her a taxi. When he got one, she jumped in, gave Cousin Felix's address and said to the driver:

'Go as quickly as you can. Hurry, please, hurry!'

'It isn't going to be easy in this traffic,' the taximan replied. 'Not unless you can turn the cab into a helicopter.'

He laughed at his own joke and Karina lay back against the seat with her eyes closed. She had got to stop Felix, she thought; somehow, in some way, she had got to stop him from using the information he had stolen from the safe.

She tried to imagine what use he could make of Garland's list of holdings. She was very vague about financial deals, but she could imagine that Garland had competitors who would like to know how many shares he held in different companies so that they could out-vote or even out-bid him.

Yet it seemed preposterous that Felix could think of competing in the world of finance of which Garland was one of the big figures. She could not understand it and yet she knew that in stealing that list Felix was in some way a deadly threat to Garland's interests.

The taxi seemed to get into one traffic block after another.

'Hurry! Hurry!' she prayed. If only she could be there in time; if only she could stop Felix from using the information that he had stolen from her by such perfidious methods.

She hated him, she thought. How could she ever have trusted him for a moment? And yet she knew that when he had come to Letchfield Park he had seemed to her, in her misery and fear, a knight in shining armour.

The traffic in the West End seemed even worse than it had been in the City. They crawled down Piccadilly, and at last turned into the side streets of Mayfair. She had the money ready in her hand when the taxi drew up outside the imposing block where Felix had his flat. She jumped out, paid the man and ran up the steps.

'Is Mr Mainwaring in?' she asked the porter.

'He came in about five minutes ago, miss,' the porter replied, smiling. He knew her by sight and she had already learned that he was a friend of Carter's.

Karina ran towards the lift.

'You'll find the door open, miss,' the porter called after her. 'Mr Carter's just stepped out to buy something and he told me he had left the door ajar because he is expecting the coalman.'

'Thank you,' Karina managed to say as the lift shot upwards towards the fifth floor. She stepped out, shutting the lift doors behind her, and went towards the smart red door with its polished brass plate, which was the entrance to Felix's flat.

Only now did she pause and feel a sudden

shyness – or was it fear – at facing Felix and accusing him of what he had done. She was conscious that her fingers were cold and that her heart was beating quickly as she pushed open the door and stood for a moment in the faint gloom of the incense-scented hall.

It was then that she heard Felix's voice. He was in the sitting-room and the door was ajar.

'Finally, twenty thousand shares in Moores and Pethering,' he was saying. 'That's rather what we thought, isn't it?'

The person at the other end of the line must have replied, and Felix went on:

'Well, it's not too bad, and if you start buying first thing Monday morning no one should suspect anything until Wednesday, at least. He's in India, so they'll have trouble in getting hold of him. You can get a plane from Zurich tomorrow and I'll meet you at the airport. It couldn't have worked out better, could it?'

There was a pause and then Felix chuckled.

'Yes,' he said. 'I can congratulate myself on being pretty astute over this. Everything went according to plan.'

Again there was a long communication from the other end and then he said:

'The secretary? Oh, I disposed of her quite cleverly – the chocolates from that man you

254

suggested. She'll be well again in a few days. She's not likely to have them analysed – people never do.'

The man on the other end of the line had a lot to say before Felix continued:

'One minute, Eric! I've got a list of those in my safe. Hold on and I'll get it for you.'

Karina suddenly awoke to the fact that he might be coming out and would see her. She turned quickly and went through a door on her left. She realised as she did so that she was in Felix's bedroom and looked round wildly for somewhere to hide. She saw another door which obviously led into the bathroom and sped across the room. She had just reached it and pulled it shut behind her when she heard Felix come into the room.

'Are you there, Carter?' he said as if he sensed there was someone about.

Karina held her breath. She heard Felix moving about. She heard various clicks which she recognised as the lock of the safe. Then she heard him go out again and his voice coming faintly from the sitting-room. She opened the bathroom door.

'I've got them,' she heard him say. 'Shall I read them out to you?'

She moved cautiously into the bedroom. Beside the mantelpiece a picture had been swung back from the wall and behind it was a safe. It was open and it also contained papers rather as Garland Holt's had done.

Karina glanced at them casually, then stood suddenly still as if turned to stone. Above the papers on another shelf, standing shining and twinkling in the light from the window, was the pink elephant which Garland had called his luck!

For what seemed to her an eternity she stared at it. From the other room Felix was still talking. Then, acting on an impulse quicker and stronger than thought, Karina ran across the bedroom floor, put her hand into the safe and drew out the pink elephant.

Just for a moment she felt it cold and heavy in her hand before she cradled it against her breast under her coat. Then, slipping out of the bedroom and through the hall, she reached the landing and rang for the lift. It came up to her with a clang and she flung open the gates. It was speeding down!

A few minutes later, breathless, her eyes wide in her white face, Karina found herself standing at the corner of the street clutching under her coat a pink quartz and jewelled elephant worth ten thousand pounds, and wondering wildly what she should do next!

CHAPTER ELEVEN

For some moments Karina stood on the pavement staring blindly at the traffic, trying to think what to do or where she should go. And then she saw a telephone-box on the other side of the road. She crossed to it and shut the door behind her.

It took her some time to thumb through the pages of the directory and find the name of the firm for which Jim worked; but at last she found it and, picking up the receiver, was just about to dial the number when across the other side of the road, through the traffic, she saw Felix.

Instinctively she shrank against the wall of the telephone-box, watching him looking up and down the road, first one way and then the other. He was hatless and she realised that he was looking for her.

Then, as the traffic cleared for a moment, she saw the expression on his face. He looked almost like a man possessed of the devil. She felt herself shrink and shiver, but she could do nothing but hold the buzzing telephone to her ear, standing there feeling the pink elephant hard against her breast and knowing, with a feeling of sick horror, that she was being hunted like an animal.

For the first time she realised what she was up against. This was no joke, no amusing incident, to the man she had just tricked out of his evil spoils. It was something far more dangerous and desperate than that.

Felix moved away a little up the street to look down another turning. Now he had his back to her, but still she could feel, even at this distance, the anger and the evil of him. He turned again, and now she felt as if the very fact that she was looking at him must draw his attention to her.

She turned her back with an effort that was almost like a physical pain. It was agony to stand there, not knowing what he was doing, not knowing if he might not be advancing towards her; to stand trembling, still with the buzzing receiver in her ear, to wait and wonder what would happen if he found her.

She thought how precarious her position was. If she disappeared, who would know or care? She was so small, so ineffectual. Felix was strong and utterly ruthless.

It seemed to her that she must have stood with her back to the road for an eternity before she peeped over her shoulder, scanning the whole street, both to the right and to the left.

Felix had gone!

But he would not have given up the

search, she was certain of that. She could not go back to her lodgings. She could not return to the office. With shaking fingers she dialled Jim's number. It was answered immediately, but it took a long time for them to find him and the minutes seemed to tick by almost like hours.

'Hello!'

It was his voice at last.

'Jim! It's Karina!'

'Don't say you are going to put me off for lunch,' he said, 'because I won't stand for it.'

'No, no, I'm not going to put you off,' Karina said. 'But something terrible has happened. Jim, I'm in trouble. Please help me.'

'Of course I'll help you,' he answered soothingly. 'What's happened?'

'I can't tell you on the telephone. Let me meet you somewhere – anywhere. I'll take a taxi.'

He didn't waste time in asking her what was the matter.

'Where are you?' he asked.

'At the corner of Curzon Street,' she answered.

'Then tell the taxi to take you to Leicester Square Tube Station,' he said. 'It's about halfway between us and I will be there at the same time as you.'

'Thank you, Jim! Thank you!'

Karina's voice broke on the relief that his

words brought her.

'Cheer up,' she heard him say. 'There's nothing so bad that it can't be mended.'

She put down the receiver, and after looking once again up and down the street she stepped out of the telephone box and ran as fast as her feet could carry her into Park Lane. There were plenty of taxis and she got one within a few seconds.

'Leicester Square Tube Station,' she said, and, getting into the taxi, sank back in the corner.

She was frightened even to look out of the window in case Felix, by some wild coincidence, should be passing by in his car or walking down the pavement.

'What would he do to me?' she asked herself, and was afraid to formulate an answer.

There was a traffic block in Piccadilly and it took nearly twenty minutes to reach Leicester Square Tube Station. But to Karina's relief, as the taxi drew up, she could see Jim standing on the pavement, his bowler hat set at a jaunty angle on his head, his rolled umbrella in his hand. He looked ridiculously and reliably English, and she felt as if all her ideas of being pursued and persecuted were just nonsense, things which didn't happen outside a green-backed thriller.

She waved and Jim stepped up to the taxi and opened the door.

'Where do you want to go?' he asked.

'Anywhere,' Karina answered. 'But I mustn't be seen. Somewhere where no one will recognise us.'

Jim gave the taxi-driver an address and got in beside her.

'What's happened?' he asked.

In answer Karina drew the pink elephant out from beneath her coat and held it out to him. He looked at it and gave a low whistle of surprise.

'Garland's luck!' he exclaimed. 'Where did you find it?'

'I ... I stole it,' Karina said.

Jim's eyes widened.

'From Garland?'

'No, no, of course not,' Karina replied, almost laughing at the idea that he should imagine she had been the original thief. 'No, from the man who must have helped steal it in the first place.'

'Who?'

Karina took a deep breath.

'Cousin Felix.'

Jim whistled again and then he said:

'Does he know that you've got it?'

Karina nodded.

'Then I understand why you don't want to be seen,' Jim said. 'Hadn't you better tell me all about it from the beginning?'

The taxi came to a standstill as he spoke and Karina looked out to see that they had

261

stopped outside the National Gallery. She looked at Jim in surprise, but he smiled at her.

'The best place to hide I know,' he said. 'You never find anyone here but students and artists.'

He paid the taxi and, taking her arm, helped her up the steps. Hastily she put the pink elephant underneath her coat again and they entered one of the long galleries and sat down on a seat. As Jim had said, there was no one about except a woman sketching at the far end of the gallery and a few rather scruffy-looking students with long hair and duffel coats.

'Tell me what it's all about,' Jim said.

Karina looked over her shoulder instinctively and he put out his hand and took hers.

'It's all right,' he said comfortingly. 'You're safe here. I promise you. I won't let anybody hurt you.'

Karina tried to smile, but her lips were trembling. She was beginning now to feel the reaction from all she had been through.

'It's all right,' Jim said again. 'Just start from the beginning.'

She told him then exactly what happened the day before when Felix had taken her out to lunch and made her repeat to him the names of the people with whom Garland had made appointments for the following week.

'I suppose I ought to have refused,' she said miserably.

'Nonsense!' Jim said. 'You couldn't do anything else in the position you were in but tell him. Go on. Why wouldn't you dine with me last night?'

She felt her face flush and was suddenly conscious that he was holding her hand very tightly.

'I ... I had a headache,' she said, unable to meet his eyes.

Jim watched her without saying anything, but she knew he was not satisfied with her explanation.

'It was better this morning,' Karina went on. 'I got up early and arrived at the office almost before anyone else.'

She told him about the cable from Garland, how Miss Weston had rung up and how ill she was, having been sick all night.

'It was Cousin Felix who was responsible for that. I heard him say on the telephone that the chocolates were responsible.'

'The sort of trick he would play!' Jim exclaimed.

'Of course, I didn't know that at the time,' Karina went on. Then she told him how she had the safe open when Felix came into the office.

'He must have timed it very cleverly,' Jim said. 'But he knew that you would have been told the combination, so that even if you had shut it he would have forced you to open it again.'

'But how did he know that I would have to get it open,' Karina enquired. 'He couldn't have known about the cable.'

'Of course he knew,' Jim replied. 'He sent it himself.'

'And pretended it was from Garland?' Karina enquired.

'Naturally,' Jim answered. 'I expect the man he is working for has got a stooge or an agent in India. It would be quite easy to instruct him to send a cable in Garland's name. Or, in all probability, you will find that the cable didn't come from India at all but from somewhere like Rome or Zurich. Miss Weston would never have suspected that it had not been sent by Garland on his way to India, she might have thought that perhaps the delivery had been delayed. Finish your story.'

Karina did so, telling how Felix had stolen the documents labelled 'Holdings'; how she had followed him to his flat, how she had overheard the conversation on the telephone and had hidden in the bathroom, seen the pink elephant in the safe and fled with it.

'Perhaps I was silly to take it,' she said. 'If I hadn't, he would never have known that anyone had been there and we could have warned Mr Holt about the other things.'

'Of course,' Jim agreed, 'but it's a little late to think about that now. What we've got to worry about is not Garland but you.'

'Me?' Karina asked.

'You know why,' Jim said simply.

'I thought that myself,' Karina replied, remembering with a shudder Felix's face as he had searched for her and peered up and down the street.

Jim was silent for a moment and she knew that he was thinking.

'We must warn Mr Holt,' Karina said. 'What harm can they do him?'

'I imagine they are going to use the knowledge of how many shares he possesses in each company either to bid for control or play the markets in some way which might make things very difficult for him,' Jim said. 'I'm not a financial expert but I bet a great many of Garland's competitors would give a good deal of money to see that particular list.'

'Can't we do anything about it?' Karina asked.

Jim shrugged his shoulders.

'Only Garland can do that.'

'Then we must telephone him,' Karina said agitatedly. 'Please, Jim, help me. How can we get through to him?'

Jim didn't answer and she went on:

'I can't bear to think that this has happened all through me. How could I have brought him such trouble and such bad luck? How can I ever explain to him how sorry I am.'

Still Jim didn't answer. She felt his hand suddenly relinquish hers and turned enquiringly to look straight into his eyes.

'You love him, don't you?' he said quietly.

There was something in the way he said it which told her more forcibly than if he had put it into words that he loved her, too.

'Yes, Jim, I do,' she answered softly.

'Does he love you?'

'Of course not. It's quite, quite hopeless. One of those things which just happen and one can't help it. He'll never know.'

Jim gave a deep sigh.

'Lucky Garland! He's always been the lucky one of the family. He's always got everything, even though he tried to pretend that I once pipped him at the post where a girl was concerned. It was all nonsense really. He's hated me for a lot of other reasons, but I've never hated him until now.'

'I'm sorry, Jim.'

'You're different, somehow, from anyone else I have ever known,' Jim said. 'I haven't been able to think of anything else since I met you. I'm going to say it, Karina, even though you don't want me to. I love you, and I mean it in a way that I've never meant it to any other woman.'

'Oh, Jim, please don't. Please don't be

266

unhappy about it,' Karina begged. 'I want to be friends with you. I want you to help me. But I can't help it that my heart feels something for Garland that I could never feel for you or for anyone else.'

'As I have said before,' Jim said bitterly, 'lucky Garland!'

Karina put her hand on his arm.

'Help me! Please help me!'

'All right,' he answered. 'It goes against the grain, but I have already thought of what you must do.'

'What?'

'Go out to him. Tell him the story yourself. Actually it kills two birds with one stone. We've got to take care of you, keep you out of harm's way, and somehow this complicated tale has got to be told to Garland. If we could get through to him on the telephone, which I very much doubt, it is going to take hours to explain, while if you saw him you could do it in a few minutes. You can also take him back his luck.'

'But how can I go to India?' Karina asked.

'The more I think of it,' Jim said, ignoring her question, 'the more I think it is the only sensible approach. If Garland knows the whole facts of the case you can bet your bottom dollar he will be able to work things out one way or another. Also he'll know better than we do who is involved in this.

You didn't hear the man's name to whom Felix was talking, by any chance?'

'No, I'm afraid not,' Karina replied. Then she gave a little exclamation. 'I heard his christian name though! Cousin Felix said, "One minute, Eric, I've got a list of those in my safe."'

'Eric!' Jim said. 'I wonder now. There's an Eric Cowley who has always been one of Garland's rivals. He's one of the big financiers and a nasty bit of work, from all I've heard. My God! I've got it! He's a collector of pictures, ivories and all sorts of things of that kind. I'm always seeing that he's paid some fabulous price for a piece of furniture at Christies or a picture at Sotheby's. I don't mind betting you that he's at the bottom of the whole thing. He's the sort of chap who would take the advice of someone like Felix Mainwaring and pay him to pull his chestnuts out of the fire for him.'

'But would he really stoop to stealing?' Karina asked.

Jim shrugged his shoulders.

'You can't understand chaps of that sort,' he said. 'They would do anything if it gave them a feeling of power or triumph. He may have wanted to get even with Garland. He may just have wanted to add to his secret collection of objects which are the only ones of their kind. Heaven knows what he thought! Garland will be able to tell you better than I can what the man is like.'

'But I can't go to India,' Karina said. 'I haven't got a passport.'

'That's another hurdle,' Jim replied. 'You don't make it easy, do you?'

'I'm sorry,' Karina said humbly.

Jim got to his feet.

'Well, come on. We'd better get cracking. Passport first, then the bookings, and lastly I expect you'll need a few clothes.'

Karina opened her bag.

'I've got exactly two pounds fourteen shillings and twopence!' she said despairingly.

Jim laughed.

'About the same amount as I've got. But a wise man once said to me, "Never let money stand in the way of opportunity!" I never have.'

He took her arm and they ran together down the steps. The fountains were playing and the pigeons were waddling about waiting to be fed. Karina suddenly felt lighthearted. It was impossible, she knew, quite impossible. And yet somehow her heart sang that she was going to India, she was going to see Garland.

Jim didn't take a taxi as she expected. Instead he led her into a small side street off the Strand. There was a photographer there advertising *Passport Photographs While You Wait*. He took her in, galvanised the man into working at double-quick time, and in what seemed to her a few minutes they had the photographs in their hands and Jim was signalling a taxi.

'Where are we going now?' Karina asked.

'To see a friend of mine,' he answered. 'And, incidentally, I'm going to ask you to be blind, deaf and dumb about all that occurs from now on. As I've said, the gentleman in question is a friend of mine and I don't want him sent to Dartmoor for a holiday?'

'You mean you are going to get me a false passport?' Karina asked.

'Unless you prefer to wait a week or so for your trip to India, it's the only possible way,' Jim answered. 'Fortunately I have friends in strange places. This man was a Commando and was with me in the war. He was damned brave and deserved the V.C, but the police would love to get their hands on him.'

The taxi stopped in a long, narrow, rather dirty street down by the Embankment. Jim, with Karina following, climbed down some crumbling steps into a basement. Jim rang the bell, and after some minutes the door was opened by a man over six feet tall wearing a cloth cap at the back of his head.

'Bless me! If it ain't the Major,' he said when he saw Jim. 'I wondered what 'ad happened to you as I'd not 'eard from you for so long. 'ow're you keeping?'

'Well enough,' Jim answered. 'And I need not ask how you are doing. I saw the Rolls-Royce outside the door.'

The man shook with laughter as if Jim had said the wittiest thing in the world.

'Come in,' he said. 'Don't stand about 'ere. We might 'ave the coppers nosing around to see 'oo me callers are. They're friendly enough, as it 'appens, at the moment. But I don't like to draw attention to meself.'

'I bet you don't,' Jim answered, leading Karina into a passage which smelt of damp and saying as he did so: 'This is Miss Burke, Bill – she's all right. I'm hoping to marry her one day, if she'll have me.'

'Well, now, isn't that nice to 'ear?' Bill exclaimed. 'Congratulations, Major; you always were a good picker. And best wishes to you, m'dear,' he added, shaking Karina by the hand. 'The Major's gold right through, I'll say that for 'im.'

'Except where my pocket's concerned,' Jim said quickly.

Karina felt embarrassed, but she said nothing. She understood only too well that Jim had to vouch for her in some way or other and this was the easiest way.

'Come into me boodwar,' Bill suggested with a grin.

He led the way down the passage and opened the door at the end. Karina was

271

surprised that the room really was comfortable. It must once have been an artist's
studio and it looked out on to a narrow
courtyard surrounded by high warehouses.
But it was light and airy and comfortably
furnished. There was a big fire burning in
the grate and a carpenter's bench covered
with all sorts of tools down one side of the
room.

'What are you working on now?' Jim said.
'Locks?'

'Anything that requires a delicate touch,
Major. That's what they always say to me.
"Nobody 'as fingers like you, Bill!"'

'You're an old blackguard,' Jim said affectionately. 'I want some help, Bill. A passport
for this lady. She's got to go to India at once
and we've not time to fulfil all Her Majesty's
regulations.'

'Well, now, isn't that a bit of luck?' Bill
exclaimed. 'I might almost 'ave known that
you were coming. I bought a passport only
last week. A girl who dived off the side of the
river – nice-looking bit of goods she was too.
On the usual job, of course!'

He winked at Jim and then coughed
politely as if he had said too much in front
of Karina.

'Now let's see,' he said quickly. 'Where did
I put it?'

He rummaged in the drawers of a rather
nice tallboy. Karina could not help seeing

272

that the drawers had a number of passports in them. She glanced enquiringly at Jim.

'Quite a good line of business,' Jim muttered almost beneath his breath with a smile.

Soft though the words were, Bill heard them.

'Not 'alf as good as it used to be. Too many countries slackening up their precautions because of the tourists. The price of fixing these things 'as dropped badly.'

'I should think that's because of too much competition,' Jim said.

'Competition!' Bill answered scornfully. 'It isn't everyone 'oo can fix them as I do, and well you know it, Major.'

'And well I know it,' Jim agreed. 'Well, come on, we haven't got all day to waste. Here are the photographs.'

He took the photographs of Karina out of his pocket and held them out.

'Trust you to forget nothing, Major,' Bill said admiringly.

He took the passport and sat down at the bench and started lifting the photograph that was already on it. Karina watched him, fascinated.

'By the way,' Jim said casually. 'We shall also want a vaccination certificate and one of those cholera and typhoid things.'

'You'll find 'em in the other drawer,' Bill said. 'Fill 'em in, Major, while I do this. Harris is the name I usually sign for the quack – H. A. Harris. There are a hundred and six of 'em in the Medical Directory.'

Jim took the papers and, drawing a pen from his pocket, started to fill them in. Karina was fascinated. When Jim had finished writing he looked up at Bill.

'Stamps?' he said. 'The official ones!'

'They're on the table somewhere,' Bill answered. 'I can't tell you what a job I 'ad, Major, cutting that rubber stamp. Took me nearly a week it did to get it right. But now no one could tell the different between mine and some desk-wallah's in Whitehall.'

Jim found the rubber stamps, pressed them on to the papers and handed them to Karina. She looked at them and her eyes widened.

'But these aren't in my name,' she said.

Jim smiled at her.

'No, Karina, but Bill's passport is a real one. You'll have to be Miss June Robinson.'

'That was the girl who died,' Karina said in a low voice.

'I don't think she would begrudge you using her passport for something as important as this,' Jim said in an understanding tone.

Bill looked up.

'That she wouldn't. She was a good sort, was June. Give away the shirt off 'er back, she would, if it'd 'elp anybody. Far too generous in some ways she was. I could tell you how…'

'That's all right, Bill,' Jim said quickly. 'Miss Burke understands.'

'Well, don't let 'er forget what 'er name is,' Bill said with a laugh. 'And make the labels on yer luggage the same. Not like one chap 'oo's passport I fixed for 'im. Goes blithely off to the Continent with all 'is labels in 'is own name. 'ad a deuce of a job explaining 'e was taking it over to oblige a friend.'

Bill laughed so much that the table seemed to shake in front of him. But he had finished what he was doing and handed Karina the passport with a little bow. He had certainly made a good job of it. Her photograph was where June Robinson's had been and the official stamp on it was quite perfect as far as the eye could see.

'Now, Major, that'll be fifty quid, please,' Bill said. 'Double to anyone else, but you know I always charge special prices for you.'

'You'll get it next week,' Jim replied quietly.

Karina saw Bill stiffen.

'Not on your nelly,' he said. 'You know my terms. Cash and no 'ard feelings.'

Jim smiled disarmingly.

'I'm sorry, Bill, but this was an emergency. I brought Miss Burke here without going home. In fact, when I came out this morning, I had no idea what was going to happen.'

Bill put his hands into his trouser pockets.

'Listen, Major. You and me 'ave been pals for a long time and I don't want to fall out with you. My terms is cash and I wouldn't give credit to the Prime Minister 'imself.'

'You know me, don't you?' Jim said. 'You know I'm always broke. But this is different. Karina, show him what you've got under your arm.'

Reluctantly, because by now she was rather afraid of Bill, Karina drew out the pink elephant. Bill put out his hand and took it from her.

'Blimey! I seem to know this – or, rather, I've 'eard of it.'

He put it down on the table and thumbed through a pile of papers.

'You needn't bother,' Jim told him. 'It's part of the lot stolen from Mr Holt's house a week ago.'

'I thought so,' Bill said.

'As it happens, Miss Burke is taking it to India to Mr Holt,' Jim explained. 'But I don't expect you to believe that. What I'm suggesting is that you take one of the stones out of it. They are all of them worth more than fifty pounds and well you know it. Hold it, and when I bring you the money you can give it back.'

'Now you're talking business, Major,' Bill smiled.

He picked up the elephant again and

turned it over in his hand.

'If I wasn't an honest man,' he said, 'I'd take the emeralds. They're worth a pretty packet. But, as it is, and seeing as it's you, Major, one of the diamonds round the base will do me.'

'I bet it will,' Jim answered. 'Any of the diamonds is well worth two or three hundred pounds. Never mind, take your choice – and mind you give me the same one back when I redeem it.'

'Major, you 'urt me with your suspicions,' Bill answered.

He gouged the diamond out with a thin delicate tool. Then Jim said quietly:

'I've got to raise the money for Miss Burke's ticket. What about lending me a hundred and fifty pounds on ten per cent interest?'

'Fifteen,' Bill said.

'All right, fifteen,' Jim agreed. 'You'd better take another couple of stones while you're about it. It'll save time.'

Bill took them out and then, drawing a key from his pocket, unlocked another drawer in the same tallboy from which he had taken the passport. He drew out a wad of notes secured with a rubber band.

'A hundred and fifty enough, Major?' he enquired.

'It will do,' Jim said. 'I can't afford any more at your disgraceful rates of interest.'

'Business is business,' Bill said laconically.

He gave Jim the money and Karina picked up the pink elephant. She felt somehow that it had been hurt by having some of its precious stones taken from it. And yet she was thankful that she had not had to leave the elephant itself in bond so as to be able to pay her way to India.

'Goodbye, Bill. I'll be seeing you,' Jim said. 'Keep those diamonds safely.'

'They'll be 'ere if I am,' Bill replied.

Jim turned towards the door through which they had entered the room, but Bill stopped him.

'Better go out the other way, Major,' he said. 'You never know 'oo's watching. Too many rich clients might make the cops think I was in the money.'

'So it might,' Jim agreed.

Bill shook them both warmly by the hand and ushered them across the courtyard and through another door which led to a narrow alleyway. A few yards took them back on to the Embankment and Jim managed to get a taxi.

'Thomas Cook's,' he said briefly.

'I can't believe it's true,' Karina said as they drove off. 'It all seems like something out of a film.'

'It's the advantage of having a disreputable past,' Jim smiled. 'You see, most people would disapprove of my friendship with someone like Bill, but he has his uses.'

'Do you think I shall be able to get on an aeroplane today?' Karina said.

'We'll manage it somehow,' Jim replied confidently. 'Do you know where Garland is?'

'He's in Delhi at the moment,' Karina answered.

They were nearing the West End and Karina sank back a little into the corner of the seat.

'You don't think that Cousin Felix might suspect I would go to him?' she asked.

'Of course he might,' Jim answered. 'But he'll find that Karina Burke has not booked a passage. Have you forgotten that June Robinson is your name from now on?'

'I'll try to remember it,' Karina replied. She drew a deep breath. 'I don't know how to thank you, Jim, for all this.'

'There's no need,' he answered.

'There is,' she protested. 'I know why you are doing it and I think it's very wonderful of you.'

'Nonsense,' he said almost roughly. 'I love you and that's that. Go and see Garland; and if he isn't what you expect or you fall out of love with him, come back quickly to me. I shall be waiting.'

'Thank you,' Karina said simply.

But she knew even as she said it that she wouldn't fall out of love with Garland. It was just one of those hopeless but undeniable things. She loved him! Loved him with her whole heart and soul, even though she knew he would never love her in return.

CHAPTER TWELVE

The aeroplane rose into a translucent blue sky. The sunshine was dazzling on its silver wings; and Karina, leaning forward in her seat, looked down and saw the white, square houses of Delhi growing smaller and smaller until they looked like bricks that a child might have played with.

Now she could see the river winding like a silver ribbon through the sun-baked brown earth which seemed to stretch away into an indeterminate distance to meet the sky.

She sat back in her seat. The pretty Indian air hostess, wearing a blue sari, asked her if she would like a newspaper, and when she shook her head, smiled at her sweetly and went on to speak to the other passengers.

It seemed unbelievable, Karina thought, that she was here in India and travelling at this moment towards Garland, getting nearer and nearer to him with every rev of the throbbing engines.

It had been a bitter disappointment when she arrived last night to find that Garland was no longer in Delhi. She had telephoned from the airport, feeling shy and embarrassed at the idea of just walking in on him.

The clerk at the Ashoka Hotel, where he had been staying, had explained helpfully that he had already left.

'Mr Holt is in Agra,' he said. 'He will be returning here on Monday if you wish to see him.'

'I am afraid that will be too late,' Karina said. 'I must see him at once.'

'I will give you his address,' the clerk said.

With the address in her hand Karina had thought of telephoning. And yet, having come so far, she felt she could not bear to struggle with explanations on the telephone. No, she must see him in person – her common sense told her that. But her heart echoed the decision for a very different reason.

All through the long hours of flying she had thought of him, feeling that in some way he must be aware that she was doing so much for his sake. Then she had told herself that she was being ridiculous. She meant nothing in Garland Holt's life, nothing. And all she was doing was merely to try to right a wrong, to save him from the trouble and financial loss which she had inadvertently been instrumental in bringing upon him.

She felt she could never be sufficiently grateful to Jim for all he had done for her. First of all he had found that there was a seat available on an aeroplane leaving London Airport late that evening.

It was while they were waiting in the lounge that suddenly over the loudspeaker had come an announcement:

'Will Miss Karina Burke come immediately to the B.O.A.C information desk,' the impersonal voice had boomed.

Karina had given a start and gone very white. Almost instinctively she started to rise, but Jim's hand had gone down quickly on her arm.

'Don't move. Don't look as if it meant anything to you,' he said. 'Karina Burke is not here, you are June Robinson. Remember that, June Robinson.'

She felt herself breathe again.

'What does it mean?' she asked.

He shrugged his shoulders.

'Merely a precaution, I imagine. He's very likely having you called every hour or every time there's a plane leaving for India.'

'Do you think he's here?'

'He may be,' he answered. 'But, anyway, don't worry. It's unlikely he'll be allowed into this inside lounge. It's only for people who are actually travelling and those who are seeing them off.'

Jim's words were reassuring, but Karina was afraid until the very last moment. Only when she could actually leave and pass through the door on to the airfield and hurry across the windy asphalt to where the plane was waiting did she feel that Felix no longer had any hold over her.

Jim had put his arms around her when her flight was announced.

'Goodbye, Karina,' he said. 'Take care of yourself. You know I will be waiting in case you come back to me.'

'I can't begin to thank you, Jim.'

'Don't try,' he answered.

She had kissed him goodbye, putting up her mouth impulsively, so grateful for all he had done, so conscious that the trip would have been impossible unless he had arranged it for her.

He kissed her desperately, the kiss of a man who sees something which means everything to him slipping out of his grasp. And then, with his gay, irresponsible smile, he had raised her hand to his lips.

'Good luck and God bless.'

She was conscious then that the tears were not far from her eyes. And as she reached the plane, she had turned and waved, seeing him, an indistinct figure through the glass windows of the waiting-room.

They were off! She really had escaped. Felix had not caught up with her; there had not been a last-minute hitch over her passport; the police had not arrived to show her up for the impostor she was.

The stewardess spoke to her as Miss Robinson and with an effort she managed to reply without looking surprised.

'June Robinson, June Robinson, June Robinson,' she repeated over and over again to herself.

She couldn't help wondering, with a sudden smile of irrepressible humour, what Aunt Margaret would say if she knew that she was flying out to India on borrowed money, with the passport of a lady of easy virtue and a stolen pink quartz elephant worth ten thousand pounds wrapped round in her nightgown.

She felt very small and lonely as the great aeroplane rose higher and higher in the sky and she saw England lying beneath her like a map of tiny fields, small villages and dolls' houses. And then she thought of Garland and knew that in sixteen hours she would see him.

She had not expected the setback of finding that he had already left Delhi. The Indian Government tourist representative was extremely kind and took her to a small, inexpensive hotel for the night. It had been dark as she drove from the airport into Delhi, and yet even the darkness was different. There was an acrid odour of wood smoke, of earth dried by the sun and the exotic fragrance of strange flowers – the smells which she had only read about in books.

The lighted streets were an enchantment. People in white clothes moved in front of the open-fronted shops, looking exactly as Karina had dreamed they would. The men sitting cross-legged before a pyramid of fried cakes, selling yards of coloured material to veiled women, or offering brightly coloured drinks to passers-by, seemed to her just like something out of a film. There was noise, confusion and dark faces with exquisite features turning to look curiously at the car with its hooting horn.

All too quickly she had arrived at the hotel and been taken up to her room. She was more tired than she had realised, and after a somewhat indifferent dinner in the dining-room, of which she was the only occupant, she went to bed.

She would have liked to walk about the streets, but she hadn't got the courage to go out alone; and she felt, too, that she must stay and guard the pink elephant until she had put it safely into Garland's hands.

The Indian Government tourist representative had arrived to fetch her at six o'clock the next morning to take her to the airport. He had also brought with him her ticket on the aeroplane to Agra. She had realised when she paid for it that she was left with only a few shillings in her purse. She hoped that Garland was still at Agra and hadn't moved on elsewhere. If he had, she would have to telephone him. There was no question of her following him any farther.

It was warm in the aeroplane, and Karina was glad that she had spent some of the precious money Jim had borrowed from Bill in buying a cotton dress. It was crisp and fresh, and the white sandals which went with it were comfortable on her feet.

The aeroplane was not full and she had no one seated beside her, which was a relief as she might have had to talk, and what she wanted to do more than anything else was to look out of the window and watch India unfold beneath her.

In only a few minutes it seemed to her the captain's voice told them to fasten their seat belts and she knew they were coming down at Agra. It was now that the very moment was upon her that she began to feel a sudden sick sense of apprehension. Would Garland be very angry? she wondered. She had seen him angry on more than one occasion, and she knew that while in the past she had been prepared to defy him, now because of her love it was going to be more difficult than it had ever been before.

There were taxis waiting at the airport. She managed to secure one and told the driver to go to the address the clerk at the Ashoka Hotel had given her.

'Very nice house,' the Sikh driver said conversationally. 'Rich man; many visitors.'

He was ready to chat all the way into Agra,

and Karina realised that he was particularly delighted because she was English.

'I serve English memsahib many years. I very sorry when the British leave India.'

Karina told him about England and her flight. At the same time her thoughts were increasingly preoccupied with the interview which lay ahead of her. It had seemed in London the obvious thing to fly out to Garland, to tell him what had happened. But now to put the story into words was a very different thing altogether.

The car turned in through stone pillars carrying wrought iron gates and round a great bed of brilliantly coloured flowers to draw up in front of an imposing-looking house with a colonnaded veranda. An Indian servant came hurrying out. Karina got out of the taxi.

'I wish to see Mr Garland Holt.'

She paid the taxi with the last rupees she had left after paying her hotel bill and followed the servant into the big hall. The air-conditioned coolness inside the house made her realise how hot she had felt since she arrived at the airport. But now there was no time to think of anything but Garland and what she was to say to him.

'One minute,' she said to the servant.

She put her suitcase down on the floor, opened it and took out the pink elephant. She had wrapped it the night before in two pieces of tissue paper. She put it under her arm.

'I will leave the suitcase here,' she said.

The servant bowed and led her through the hall and down a long passage. He opened a door at the far end. The room was furnished in English fashion with bright chintzes, comfortable sofas and chairs. A man was sitting at a desk in the window writing, with his back towards the door.

'A lady to see you, Sahib,' the servant said.

'Mr Ascher is in the garden.'

'For you, Sahib.'

Garland Holt turned round then almost irritably. He saw Karina, and the astonishment on his face would have been amusing if she had not felt so frightened, so helpless and vulnerable.

She heard the doors close behind her. She was alone with Garland, and he was staring at her as if he was seeing a ghost.

'Karina! What in the world are you doing here?' he managed to say at last.

'I had to see you.'

'To see me?'

'Yes.'

She felt as if she must force every word from her lips.

There seemed to be a sudden constriction of her throat and the thumping of her heart seemed to be echoed by a throbbing in her head.

'I don't understand. Why are you here? What has happened?'

He came towards her, forceful, masterful, just as she remembered him – not the idealised man she had been imagining all this time since she had loved him, but Garland himself – dynamic, overpowering, difficult and frightening.

She felt as if her feet would not move, would not carry her towards him. And then, impulsively, as if it explained everything, she took the pink elephant wrapped in its tissue paper from underneath her arm and held it out to him.

'I ... brought you ... this,' she said, scarcely above a whisper.

He took it from her wonderingly, stripped off the tissue paper and saw the pink elephant.

'Good God!'

He stared at it as if he could not believe it was real. And then he said:

'Where did you get it? Why have you brought it? Did the police find out who had taken it?'

His questions were shot at her in a staccato manner like a machine-gun.

'Cou-Cousin F-Felix took it,' she stammered, feeling as if she herself was guilty.

Garland glanced at her from under his eyebrows.

'I imagined he had something to do with

it. How did they catch him?'

'They didn't, if you mean the police,' Karina replied. 'I ... I stole it from him.'

'And brought it out to me,' Garland questioned. 'It seems incredible. But sit down, won't you? You'd better tell me all about it from the beginning.'

'There's something else,' Karina said.

'Yes?'

His very tone was uncompromising.

'He took the copy of your list of holdings from the safe in your office. He telephoned them to a man whose christian name is Eric who was in Zurich. He told him to come to London by aeroplane so that he could start buying on Monday. But that is why I am here. It's only Sunday today. They can't do anything until tomorrow morning.'

'The copy of my holdings!' Garland repeated. 'But how did he get into the safe? How did he know the combination?'

'Miss Weston gave it to me,' Karina answered. 'She was ill. You had cabled for the notebooks and so I had to open the safe.'

'I cabled for the notebooks? I haven't sent a cable of any sort since I've left England,' Garland snapped. 'What is all this nonsense? What's going on? Has Miss Weston gone off her head?'

'She ... she was very ill,' Karina said, 'and the cable came. Perhaps it wasn't from you.

I think Cousin Felix must have sent it, but we thought it was from you and so I went to get them out. At that moment he came into the office and ... collapsed. While I was getting some water, he stole the list of holdings.'

She went on with an effort.

'I went to his flat and heard him talking to this man on the telephone. He took something out of his safe without realising I was there. But I saw the pink elephant, so I stole it and ... and came out here to tell you.'

'I've never heard such a story in the whole of my life!' Garland exclaimed. 'And how did you manage to get here?'

'I flew,' Karina said.

'I imagined that,' he drily. 'But the money! Where did you get the money from? Did you get that from your Cousin Felix?'

'No, Jim got it for me,' Karina replied. 'I had to have a passport and we paid for it by letting the man have some of the diamonds from the base of the elephant. He's keeping them and as soon as I can repay him he will give them back.'

'Jim! What has Jim got to do with all this?' Garland enquired.

'He has been so kind. I couldn't have got here without him.'

'So Jim was mixed up in it too!' Garland said in the sarcastic, bitter voice that she disliked so much. 'I might have guessed that. Trust Jim to get in on any unsavoury business, whatever it might be. Well, I'm glad you found him useful.'

'How can you speak about him like that?' Karina asked, stung by his tone. 'It was Jim who did everything to help me get to you, so that I could warn you.'

'When I want Jim's assistance, I'll ask for it,' Garland Holt retorted. 'I've never heard such a mad, cock-and-bull story in all my life. I'd better try and get through on the telephone to Miss Weston to see if she can talk sense. As for all this stealing and re-stealing and Felix Mainwaring being allowed into my private safe, I think the whole world must have gone mad – and you included!'

He strode across the room as he spoke and picked up the telephone on the desk.

Karina felt the tears in her eyes overflow and run down her cheeks. It was not only what he had said to her, it was the way he had said it – the roughness in his tone, the anger in his eyes. She felt she could bear no more.

Half blindly, because of her tears, she walked across the room just as Garland began to explain that he wanted a personal call to England, to a Miss Weston. She opened the door and let herself out into the passage. She walked down it and came to the hall. The servant who had shown her in picked up her suitcase.

'The memsahib will require a taxi?' he enquired.

Karina shook her head and took the suitcase from him.

'I will ... walk,' she managed to say, her voice broken with tears.

She made no attempt to wipe them away. It didn't seem to matter any more. She walked out into the hot sunshine, past the brilliantly coloured flowers, down the shady drive and on to a road lined with trees.

She had no idea where she was going. She only wanted to get away from Garland. She felt it would break her heart if she had to hear his voice speaking to her again with that tone of contempt. Every word had been a stab of pain. Every word only twisted her heart the more thoroughly because she loved him so deeply.

The suitcase was heavy and it was very hot. She walked on. She saw some cars and carriages ahead of her, wondered why they were stationed there and looked up to see a notice, *'The Taj Mahal'*.

A sudden flicker of interest aroused her and came like a shaft of light through her misery. Whatever happened to her, she must see this before she left India.

She remembered how as a child she had pored over the pictures of it; how she had read about its beauty and thought that perhaps one day she would be able to visit it. Here, to her at any rate, was the most beautiful thing in the world. She would not go without seeing it.

Nobody took any notice of her as she walked up the steps and through a gateway. There were Indians selling postcards and small replicas; there were a few tourists and many visitors from other parts of India. But no one spoke to her or worried her as she pushed her way through the crowd.

And then quite unexpectedly she saw the Taj Mahal. It was even more beautiful than she had imagined. Pink and opalescent against the blue sky, it seemed as if it was just about to take off on a magic carpet.

She went down the steps towards it. There was the long row of cypress trees reflected in the water which, with its fountains, carried the eye towards the perfection of the Taj Mahal itself.

She did not go straight towards it. Instead she turned aside, finding a seat on the green lawn which lay on either side of the cypress trees. She sat down and stared at the round dome and the exquisite minarets.

'It was built for love,' she told herself. And she knew that it would always remain to her a memory of her own lost love – a love that was unattainable for her as Mumtaz Mahal had been to Shah Jahan who had built this wonder as a memorial to her.

It was so beautiful that the very beauty of

it seemed to seep into Karina's whole being. It was so beautiful that she felt herself a part of its beauty and its sorrow. And then, because she could bear neither its beauty nor her own unhappiness any longer, she began to cry.

She had covered her face with her hands and the tears were trickling through her fingers, when suddenly she heard someone say her name.

'Karina!'

She didn't move. She didn't even look up. Then she felt him sit down beside her and his arm go around her shoulders.

'Don't, Karina. Don't cry like that.'

'I c-can't help ... it,' she said in a sobbing, childish voice. 'It's so ... so ... b-beautiful and he must ... have been so ... unhappy – as unhappy as ... I am.'

'Who?' Garland asked.

She answered:

'He ... loved her and ... and he lost her.'

Her tears broke out afresh. Somehow nothing seemed to matter now but her own unhappiness and the sadness of the Taj Mahal.

'Stop crying! Stop!' Garland cried. 'I can't bear it, Karina, don't cry like that. I beg of you, or you'll make me cry too.'

She was so incredulous at what she heard that she opened her eyes and looked up at him, the teardrops glistening on the end of her eyelashes, her mouth quivering with the intensity of her grief. She saw then his face very close to hers and realised almost with a sense of shock that she had been talking to him almost without realising who he was.

'Oh, you baby, you child!' he exclaimed. 'How could I be unkind to you when I love you so utterly?'

'It is all a dream,' Karina thought. 'He cannot be saying these things. It must be something to do with the magic of the Taj Mahal.' She was hypnotised or caught up into another world. Perhaps she was dead and she didn't know it.

'I love you!' Garland said again. 'You've driven me mad. Do you think I haven't been thinking of you and Jim together every moment since I left England? I've tortured myself with visions of him kissing you, being so gay and amusing. And then, when you came here just when I was thinking of you, praising him and telling me how much he has done for you, I lost my temper. Forgive me, Karina. It was good and brave of you to come all this way to tell me what has happened. I wanted to thank you, but somehow this damned temper of mine always makes me do the wrong thing.'

'Y-you ... l-love me?'

She could hardly say the words and yet they were said and he heard them.

'Of course I love you,' he said, with something of his old arrogance. 'I have loved you since I first saw you, since that night on the balcony in Belgrave Square when I tried to find out who you were and nobody could tell me. But I know what you think of me,' he added with a rueful smile... 'The last man on earth whom you would ever marry.' He gave a deep sigh. 'It's all right, Karina. I didn't mean to worry you. But you looked so pathetic sitting there crying and it all came out before I could stop it.'

'You love me!' she repeated.

'Yes, I love you,' he answered. 'So much so that if you look at me like that I cannot hold myself responsible for not going on telling you so or from trying to kiss you, Karina, as I kissed you once before.'

'Why didn't you tell me?' she asked.

'Would it have made any difference?' he replied. 'It's Jim you are fond of, isn't it?'

She shook her head. The tears still in her eyes, they seemed to make a rainbow over his head which also encircled the domes and minarets of the Taj Mahal.

'No,' she answered. 'I told Jim that I didn't love him. He knows that ... I ... I love ... y-you.'

She felt Garland stiffen beside her. She felt him hold his body rigid.

'Say that again,' he commanded. 'Say it in case I didn't hear it aright. I warn you, Karina, if you are not telling me the truth, you are playing with fire.'

She put her hands out towards him.

'It ... it is the truth. Oh, Garland, I didn't know it, but I have loved y-you for a long time. But I ... I ... thought that you would never love anybody, least of all ... m-me.'

'You little idiot! I was waiting for you. That's why I couldn't love anybody else.'

He pulled her almost roughly towards him and then it seemed as if something broke within him and in a voice shaken and quite unlike his usual self he said:

'Be kind to me, Karina. I've never known real love and tenderness and I'm afraid of it.'

She had no words to answer this. She could only put up her little hand and touch the side of his face. He covered it with his own, kissing the palm passionately, lingeringly, with lips that seemed hungrily possessive. Then he looked down at her again.

'I have imagined you here,' he said. 'Imagined you in India ever since I arrived. I thought that perhaps one day I might be able to bring you here as my companion, as my secretary, in some way or another. I never thought that you would come as my wife.'

'Oh, Garland!'

The words were hardly above a whisper.

'You will marry me, won't you, Karina?'

he asked. 'Now, at once. Why should we wait?'

'There are a lot of things to do first,' she replied. 'All that trouble waiting for you at home.'

'What trouble?' he asked. 'Oh yes, of course! Well, I have just heard something which I think solves everything.'

He spoke impatiently, as if it was really of no account and he could hardly waste the time talking about it.

'What have you heard?' Karina asked.

'Just after you left me,' he said, '–oh, Karina, how could you run away like that? – my host came in to say he had heard on the radio that there had been an air disaster to one of the planes travelling from Zurich to London. He thought I might be interested as there were several important British people aboard. Amongst them was a man called Eric Cowley.'

'He was killed?' Karina enquired.

'They were all killed,' Garland answered. 'That only leaves me Felix Mainwaring to deal with.'

There was something in his voice which made Karina say quickly:

'Don't be cruel to him. If he can't hurt you, what does it matter? There has been so much unhappiness and greed and cruelty around us, don't add to it.'

'It shall be as you say,' Garland said quite

humbly. 'Don't you understand, Karina? I only want to do what you want. If you want me to let him go, I will do so. He can even keep the things he has stolen for Cowley. But he can't have the pink elephant because you brought it to me. You brought me back my luck, Karina. You've brought yourself, which is all that matters.'

'I can't believe it's true,' Karina said.

She still felt as if she must wake up. She couldn't really be sitting here with Garland's arms around her in this beautiful, peaceful garden, the Taj Mahal just in front of them. It still seemed to glow like a pearl, but it was no longer sad. The message it gave her now was one of happiness.

'You are so sweet,' she heard Garland say, and she looked up at him.

'Is it really true?' she asked. 'You do love me? We are together? This isn't a dream?'

'It is a dream we will go on dreaming for the rest of our lives together,' he answered.

She felt his arms tighten about her. She felt his hand underneath her chin, lifting her face towards his. And then his lips were on hers, his mouth no longer brutal and rough as it had been before, but gentle, tender and passionate with a new love and a new understanding.

She felt a sudden flame shoot through her body; she felt as if he drew her like a magnet into his keeping and that he would never let

301

her go. She felt her lips respond to his and knew that this was a love which would never alter or grow less.

She felt him draw her closer still until they were one; indivisible – one heart, one soul, one love for all eternity.

The publishers hope that this book has given you enjoyable reading. Large Print Books are especially designed to be as easy to see and hold as possible. If you wish a complete list of our books please ask at your local library or write directly to:

Magna Large Print Books
Magna House, Long Preston,
Skipton, North Yorkshire.
BD23 4ND

This Large Print Book, for people
who cannot read normal print,
is published under the auspices of

THE ULVERSCROFT FOUNDATION